All In

All In

Monique Polak

James Lorimer & Company Ltd., Publishers
Toronto

James Lorimer & Company Ltd. acknowledges the support of the Ontario Arts Council. We acknowledge the support of the Government of Canada through the Book Publishing Industry Development Program (BPIDP) for our publishing activities. We acknowledge the support of the Canada Council for the Arts for our publishing program. We acknowledge the support of the Government of Ontario through the Ontario Media Development Corporation's Ontario Book Initiative.

Cover design: Clarke MacDonald

Library and Archives Canada Cataloguing in Publication

Polak, Monique

All in / Monique Polak. (SideStreets)

ISBN 10 1-55028-913-6 (bound)

ISBN 13 978-1-55028-913-8 (bound)

ISBN 10 1-55028-912-8 (pbk.)

ISBN 13 978-1-55028-912-1 (pbk.)

    I. Title. II. Series

PS8631.O43A64 2006   jC813'.6   C2006-900998-8

James Lorimer
& Company Ltd., Publishers
317 Adelaide St. W., Suite 1002
Toronto, Ontario
M5V 1P9
www.lorimer.ca

Distributed in the
U.S. by:
Orca Book Publishers
P.O. Box 468
Custer, WA USA
98240-0468

Printed and bound in Canada

For Erica Lighter,
who has the biggest heart I know.

Acknowledgements

I needed a lot of help on my poker game to write this book. So thanks to my first poker teachers, Matthew and Jonathan Glickman, and to my regular poker "buddies" Ryan Abrams, Corey Krakower and Rachel Rudolf. Ryan, Corey and Rachel were also kind enough to agree to read the first draft of this project. Corey deserves further credit for coming up with the book's title and for showing me the ins and outs of online gambling (even though I never lost ten dollars so quickly). Thanks to Jeffrey Derevensky of McGill University's International Centre for Youth Gambling Problems and High-Risk Behaviors for sharing some of his research; Winnie Tom for details about the Asian community in

Montreal; Lee Rovinescu for sharing his experience at a private high school; Brian Smith for helping me with basketball stuff; Anthony Bossy for reviewing the sections on basketball; Jordan Frankel for having a friend who had a friend who knew how to make false IDs; and Daniel Haberman for explaining how to import information on a computer. More thanks to my dad Maximilien Polak and my friend Donna Tolmatch for reading the first draft. As always, thanks to my pals Viva Singer and Barbara Vininsky for their unflagging friendship. I'm also grateful to the team at James Lorimer: Hadley Dyer, my oh-so-smart editor; Jennifer Fox in promotion, Ryan Day in production, and James Lorimer for allowing me to write the book I wanted to write. And thanks from the deepest part of my heart to my Mr. Wonderful, Michael Shenker, and my daughter Ali, for their love, support and humour

Chapter 1

"Wanna bet?"

"There's no way he'll grade it," I tell Rick.

We're in the cafeteria, sitting at one of the long tables by the window. We don't need to check the blackboard to know what's for lunch. The whole first floor smells like roast chicken, which means open-face chicken sandwiches with gravy.

We just got out of English. Cooper gave us another of his whacked-out assignments. Do something alone you'd never usually do alone, then write about it. Observe an anthill, then write about it. Send your parents a thank-you note, then write about it.

Now, because we're reading *Alice's Adventures in Wonderland*, he wants us to sit in front of a mirror and ask ourselves, "Who in the world are you?" — and then, you guessed it, write about it.

The thing about Cooper is he only grades some

of our assignments. "My way of keeping you people on your toes," he tells us in his booming voice, the top of his bald head shining like a full moon. If you ask me, he's just lazy.

"I think it's a cool assignment," I hear Claire Labelle say. She's sitting at the next table, her pale blonde hair shimmering in the sunshine. She doesn't notice when I turn to look at her. Guys like me don't register on Claire Labelle's radar.

"So, Todd. Are you going to do Mr. Cooper's mirror assignment, or are you going to fake it, like usual?" Lewis asks, nudging me with his elbow.

I nudge him back, only a little harder than I need to. Lewis winces.

"Hey man!" he says, shaking out his elbow. "I was just asking."

"When I look at my reflection," I say, leaning back in my chair so I'm balancing on its back legs, "I see one seriously handsome dude. A dude who thinks your assignments, Cooper, are full of ..." I check to see that Miss Taylor, who's on lunch duty at the other end of our table, isn't listening. "Crap. A dude who's got way better things to do with his time than your dumb-ass homework assignments."

Lewis and Rick crack up. When Rick laughs, his eyes, which are almond-shaped and set wide apart, seem to disappear.

"You really gonna write that?" Rick asks when he stops laughing.

"Something like that," I tell him. "One thing's for sure: There's no way I'm gonna sit in front of a mirror for twenty minutes like some dork and stare at my face."

Rick reaches into his backpack and takes out a water bottle. "Drink up," he says, dropping his voice. "This'll make the chicken and gravy taste better."

I take a swig. The vodka burns as it goes down my throat. "Thanks, man," I tell him, licking my lips. "How ya doing today, Miss Taylor?" I ask, waving when I spot her looking in our direction.

Unlike Lewis and me, and most of the other kids in Grade 10, Rick is new at Hilltop. But he hasn't had trouble fitting in. The red Audi A4 convertible he keeps parked in the lot at Costa's down the street from school helps. The fact that all he has is a learner's permit and isn't supposed to drive unsupervised doesn't stop him from driving that baby all over town like he's Michael Schumacher.

"Did you get your quadratics homework done?" Lewis asks me when the waiter comes around with our trays of food. Clouds of steam rise from the chicken and the scoops of mashed potatoes. "It's due today."

"Shoot," I say, slapping my thigh under the table. "It totally slipped my mind. I'll bet you did yours though, right Lew?"

"I *always* do my homework," Lewis says, unfolding his white linen napkin and spreading it out neatly on his lap. Lewis treats every meal — even lunches at Hilltop — like it's a gourmet experience. No wonder his gut jiggles like an old man's.

11

He leans over the table and drops his voice. "You can copy mine after lunch."

"You're my man, Lew," I tell him as the waiter puts my plate down in front of me.

It's not that I'm bad at school. It's that I couldn't care less about Alice's adventures, or quadratics, or Louis Riel. I don't understand how any of that relates to my life — and I really can't imagine how it'll relate to my future. And isn't that the Hilltop motto? "Preparing young people for a bright future"?

It doesn't help that I have trouble concentrating in class. I have the kind of mind that wanders. It's part of my charm. Cooper is talking about how Alice is entering a new world when she falls down the rabbit hole, and that reminds me of this brown rabbit I used to see outside when I was a kid — before we moved to our condo. I never figured out who owned the rabbit, but he must've belonged to somebody. How else could he have survived the long, cold Montreal winters?

Or I look over at Claire Labelle and I start wondering what it'd be like to kiss her — or what she'd look like naked.

After lunch, when we're downstairs at our lockers collecting our books for math, Lewis hands me his quadratics homework and a blank sheet of lined paper. Right now, even copying his answers feels like too much work.

"You're going to help me, too, right Todd?" Lewis asks as I scribble down the answers.

You could say I'm Lewis's tutor.

I may suck in English and math and history, but I'm a wiz at Texas Hold 'em. I have been ever since I first learned to play at camp five years ago, when I was ten.

And though I'll admit there's luck involved, poker takes brains — which proves I've got them when I'm interested in a subject. To do well at poker, you need to understand human nature. You need to know when's a good time to bluff, and you need to be able to tell when one of the other guys is bluffing.

The weird thing is I'm totally focused when I play poker. That's how Lewis must get when he's doing math — or eating. When I'm playing poker, not even Claire Labelle could distract me. Okay, maybe if she was naked.

Let's just say Lewis doesn't have my natural aptitude for poker. Which is why I've been giving him lessons. Teaching him everything I know.

I'm getting up from the stairwell where I've been copying Lewis's answers, when Rick walks by and swipes me on the side of the head.

"Hey," he says, "I hear you're a pretty good poker player. Why don't you come over to my place Friday after school for a game?"

I've heard rumours Rick and his friends are really into poker.

"You can bring your sidekick," Rick says, lifting his chin in Lewis's direction. Then he turns around to make sure no one else is listening.

13

"You'll need cash," he says.

Lewis starts mumbling something, but I give him a glare that shuts him right up.

"Cool," I say, "we're in."

Chapter 2

"The guy to the left of the dealer's the small blind."

"Small blind," Lewis repeats under his breath. I can tell he's concentrating from the way his forehead's all scrunched up. You'd think there was going to be a test on this stuff.

"The guy to the left of the small blind's the big blind."

Lewis nods.

"The goal's to win the pot. That happens if you have the best cards — or if all your opponents fold. The rarer your hand, the more valuable it is. If you and your opponent are tied, the highest-ranking kicker takes the pot. The kicker's the..."

"Other card in your hand," Lewis says, finishing my sentence.

"You got it," I tell him.

Lewis smiles.

It's Wednesday after school, and we're sitting at the glass and chrome coffee table in my living room. As usual, besides us, nobody's home. My parents are at the office, and Mr. Wonderful — that's what I call my older brother Mark — has been away at school since September. He's at MIT in Boston on a full scholarship.

Not that there's much to miss. The guy basically lived in front of his computer. If that's what it takes to get a scholarship to some Ivy League school, I'll pass.

We live in this huge condo on the edge of Mount Royal. It's actually two condos — my parents had some of the walls broken down to turn it into one. They bought here because of the location. It's in Outremont, a ritzy old neighbourhood where Pierre Elliott Trudeau, who used to be prime minister, was raised. Also, it's just five minutes from our place to Hilltop.

Mr. Wonderful went to Hilltop, too. So did my dad, and so did his dad. "Made me what I am today," my dad's always saying. I guess that means Hilltop gets the blame for making my dad the kind of businessman who makes piles of money, but doesn't have a single friend on planet Earth — unless you count the people who work for him. And it's not like they have much of a choice.

"Let's see your poker face," I tell Lewis.

Lewis chews on his lower lip.

"Don't do that," I say, rolling my eyes. "It makes you look nervous."

"I am nervous."

"The trick is to look confident," I tell him, "even if you've got the lousiest hand in history."

"Show me."

I let my chin jut out a bit, and then I give this little nod. My lips touch, but I'm careful not to purse them together. Tight lips are another sign of nervousness. So's a big, goofy smile — and any kind of tapping. Guys who tap their fingers on the table, or their feet on the floor, usually have something to hide. Unless, of course, you have an amazing hand and you're just pretending to be nervous so the other guys'll keep betting. Poker's like life; it gets complicated sometimes.

"Ready to play for real?" I ask Lewis.

"You mean for money?"

"Well, we've got to practice, don't we?"

"How much do you think we need to bring to Rick's on Friday?" Lewis asks.

"A couple of hundred at least," I tell him. "Each."

Lewis makes a gulping sound. "That's, like, all I've got left from last summer. I'm not giving that up. I mowed like a hundred lawns for that."

"Relax, my man," I tell him, patting his arm. "You and me are gonna make money. Besides, can't you get some off your parents?"

"They wouldn't like it if they knew."

I shrug my shoulders. Sometimes Lewis can be a real wuss.

"Who says they have to know?"

I fan the cards out in my hands before shuffling them. Then I deal us each two cards. "Yes!" I say when I see I've got a pair of tens. When Lewis takes another bite of his lower lip, I glare at him.

"Oops," he says, catching himself. "It's a little stressful when your opponent is calling out 'Yes!' like that."

"How do you know I'm not bluffing?"

Lewis's forehead goes all scrunchy again.

"Okay," I tell him. "You're the small blind. How much you gonna bet?"

"I'll bet a buck," Lewis says.

"I'll raise you another four and bet five."

I burn a card, putting it face down in the middle of the table. "Okay, now I'm putting down the flop," I tell him as I turn over three cards. "The flop's the first three community cards. That means we each get to combine the two cards in our 'pockets' to make a five-card hand."

One of the cards in the flop is the ten of spades.

"Study the flop and figure out what you can use," I tell Lewis.

"None of those cards help me. I give up. You won." Lewis turns his cards over on the coffee table. He's got a two of spades and a king of hearts.

"Never ever do that!" I tell him, my voice rising. I'm trying to be patient, but he's not making this easy.

"What'd I do?"

"Never ever let your opponent see your cards."

"Why not?" Lewis sounds puzzled.

"Because it shows how you play. And more importantly, it shows how you think."

Lewis collects his cards from the table.

"Besides," I tell Lewis. "That was just the flop. There were still two more community cards coming: one in the turn, and one in the river. I'm thinking how it'd be better if you sat out the games at Rick's house on Friday."

"You're probably right," he says, sounding relieved. I don't think I could stand to see him lose all that hard-earned lawn-mowing money of his. On the other hand, some of that money's now mine.

"You owe me eleven bucks," I tell him, leaning back into the sofa.

He looks up at me with that sad puppy-dog look he sometimes gets.

"I thought you raised the bet to five."

"No way — I said ten."

I try not to smirk when he hands over the cash. It's a good thing I've perfected my poker face.

* * *

The condo feels really quiet after Lewis leaves. Olive, our housekeeper, has left me a plate of pasta salad and sausages for supper. There's something pathetic about being alone in your kitchen and unwrapping the plastic from a plate of food. I'm actually starting to feel bad about the extra five bucks I scammed from Lewis. I don't know why I did it. Probably because I could.

I open the cupboard to get a glass. There's a mirror hanging on the inside of the cupboard door. It's the kind that belongs in someone's locker, only my mom uses it to check her lipstick before she and Dad rush off to the office in the morning. When the mirror wobbles, I raise my hand to keep it from falling off its hook. What do they say about broken mirrors? Seven years bad luck, right?

I move in a little closer to adjust the mirror, make sure it's secure. For a second, I catch my own dark eyes, and I'm startled. Then I stop and examine my reflection. In a weird way, it feels like I've never seen myself before. Like I've never really looked.

There's a pad of flowery paper on the counter with the words "Shopping List" printed on top in fancy lettering. I reach for a pencil and jot down the thoughts that pop into my head.

I start off by writing, "Who am I, Mr. Cooper? Well I'm not exactly teacher's pet, *that's for sure*." That makes me laugh, and when I laugh, my eyes close for a second. The weird thing is, when my eyes are shut, I see the guy in the mirror. Me.

I open my eyes and pick up the pencil. "I've got my dad's eyes, my mom's protruding chin, and thank goodness, no zits like Mark had when he was in Grade 10. I'm five-foot-eight, and I've got a decent build. But there's more to me."

I put down my pencil and stare some more at

my reflection. Then I start writing again: "I'm a disappointment to my parents. I'm not a computer wiz like Mr. Wonderful, and I don't have school smarts the way Lewis does. I don't really care about anything — except poker. I'm not even a good friend. If I were, I wouldn't be ripping off the one guy I've hung out with since Grade 1."

What I write next surprises me.

"I'm scared. Scared I'll never amount to anything."

I look up from the piece of paper and into the mirror again. Only this time, I turn away. I look down at what I've written. Then I tear the piece of paper into tiny shreds and toss them into the trash.

There's no way I'd let Cooper read that.

Chapter 3

Rick's got the life.

No parents on his back telling him what to do, what time to be home, or to apply himself more in school. His mom and dad live in Hong Kong, but they wanted him and his brother to be educated in Canada. So the parents bankroll the whole deal — the fancy house, the convertibles. Probably even the poker games.

Lewis whistles as we walk to the front door, past a stone fountain with angels.

"This is some house," he says, when Rick opens the door. Rick isn't wearing his school uniform, but he's still dressed kind of formally in grey slacks and a white cashmere sweater. And silver Ray-Ban sunglasses that wrap around his head. His inky black hair is spiked at the front.

"My parents bought it because of the address," Rick says, reaching out to shake my hand.

"888 Mountainview," I say. "I guess it's easy to remember."

"Not just that," Rick says, smiling. "Chinese believe eights are lucky."

The others are already here. There's Thomas and George, two guys Rick knows from Hong Kong. Poor suckers go to Drake House, an all-boys private school in Westmount. They never get to see the likes of girls like Claire Labelle, except maybe on weekends — or in their dreams.

Thomas and George are sitting at a felt-covered poker table in the front room. We shake hands hello. They're wearing sunglasses, too, so I take mine out of my pocket and put them on. A lot of poker players wear sunglasses. Not only because they look cool, but also because they make it harder for people to guess what you're thinking.

"He's not playing," I say, gesturing over my shoulder at Lewis.

"Why not?" Thomas asks. He sounds irritated.

"Because I'm still learning," Lewis says. He puffs up his chest when he talks, but I can tell he's embarrassed. "Listen … if you guys don't want me here, I can always lea…" Lewis lets his voice trail off.

I don't say anything. I figure I'll just see how things play out.

"No way, man," Rick says, unfolding a metal chair for Lewis. "You're not leaving. Don't let these guys give you a hard time."

I take a quick look around before I sit down,

too. The Lees must have gutted the place before they moved in. There don't seem to be any walls separating the rooms on the first floor — just round cream-coloured pillars. I can see all the way into the kitchen, which is filled with gleaming appliances, and from there, out to the deck. It's like a jungle back there, with plants in huge gold pots on the ground and suspended in the air.

Maybe it's the red-and-gold material on the couches and chairs that makes the house feel Asian. But the snacks on the counter by the poker table are pure North America. Pretzels, chips, jelly beans, and of course, beer. Lots of it. Lewis helps himself to a handful of jelly beans.

"What does that say?" he asks, chomping on the candy and pointing up at the Chinese lettering on a huge red silk mural.

"That means 'Luck arrives'," Thomas explains.

"Well, that works," I tell them. "I just walked in, didn't I?"

Rick and his friends don't laugh. Truth is, I don't really believe in luck; I believe in skill. When it comes to Texas Hold 'em, if you've got skill, you make your own luck.

George tears open the bag of pretzels and eats some. "So you ready to play?" he asks me. Even though he's wearing sunglasses, I can feel him sizing me up.

Rick takes a handful of poker chips and runs them through his fingers like they're liquid, not plastic. It's a trick I've only seen on TV, but I try not to act impressed. In poker, you never want to give the other guy the upper hand, not even for a second.

"We each put in fifty bucks," Rick says. "Winner takes all. You okay with that, Todd?"

I try not to let on that I've never played for more than ten or fifteen dollars before. So the rumours are true — Rick and his pals are high rollers. I make a point of not looking at Lewis, who's sitting next to me.

Rick deals each of us two cards. I get an eight and a jack. They're offsuit; the eight's an eight of diamonds; the jack, a spade. Not great, but not a disaster either.

George is the little blind. "I'll bet ten chips," he says, putting his two cards face down on the table.

I'm the big blind. I lean back in my chair and smile — but not too much.

"I'll call and raise you to twenty," I say.

Rick wins the first hand. He had pocket aces, and another ace came out on the flop, and the fourth one in the river. When he wins the second hand and I'm down forty chips, I start wondering about all the red-and-gold lucky charms in the house. Maybe Rick and his family are on to something.

"Hey man," Lewis says, tapping Rick on the shoulder. "Any more pretzels?"

Rick bristles. "Don't touch my shoulder. It's bad luck."

"Bad luck?" Lewis says. "You're kidding, right?"

"It's a Chinese thing," George explains. "Never touch a guy's shoulders when he's playing cards."

"Sorry," Lewis says, inching his chair away from Rick's. "But what about the pretzels?"

Rick gets up and goes to the kitchen for more pretzels. When he sits back down at the table, he takes a swig of his beer.

Eight might be Rick's lucky number, but mine's five. I gain some of my chips back during the third and fourth hands, but I kill Rick in the fifth.

Thomas and George have folded, so it's just Rick and me, head to head. All I've got is a pair of nines, and there are three diamonds in the community — the common cards, the ones the dealer turned over in the flop and the river — but I'm gonna bluff.

I lean into my chair and let my belly soften. I want Rick to think I'm relaxed and confident.

"I'm all in," I say as I put all my chips into the pot.

I can hear Lewis breathing hard. Poor guy is more nervous than me.

Rick studies his cards, takes a deep breath, then throws them on the table.

"I fold," he says. He's got a pair of queens and a pair of eights. "I figured you had the flush," he adds. When Rick takes off his sunglasses, he wipes the side of his nose. I like knowing I made him sweat.

The pot's worth $150 and it's all mine. Right

now, I'm feeling like I'm king of the world. Not just because of the cash, but also because I'm good. Because I'm a winner.

"Guess you guys need a little more of that Chinese luck of yours," Lewis says when we get up to leave.

"Shut up you assh —" Thomas says, lifting himself up from his chair and making a fist with one hand.

"He's only kidding," I say, pulling Lewis out of Thomas's path. "The guy's got a weird sense of humour."

"I've gotta give it to you, Todd, you're a pretty good poker player," Rick tells me as he walks us to the door.

"Thanks, man," I say. "We should play again some time."

"Definitely," Rick says, winking at me.

One thing is bothering me though: I don't quite get why Rick folded. "I mean, what were the chances of me having a flush?" I ask Lewis on the way home.

"It's you, man, you're really good. You totally fooled him," Lewis says, and he gives me a look like I just scored a touchdown or got picked for valedictorian.

Lewis is right. I'm good. Really good.

Chapter 4

It's Sunday afternoon and I'm supposed to be studying Canadian history. I keep reading the words on the page, but nothing's sinking in. It's all just a blur of explorers. I start thinking how maybe, if I get some exercise, I'll be able to concentrate better. I could go for a run, but then I decide it'd be less effort just to go for a swim downstairs. So I change out of my jeans and into my swim trunks, and grab a towel on my way out.

You get to the pool from the back of our lobby. The pool and the area around it were designed by some fancy French architect. You'd think you were someplace like Saint-Tropez. There are palm trees and this piped-in music that's supposed to help you relax. Some days the place is overrun by rug rats splashing and shrieking. Today, luckily, I have the pool to myself.

I dive in and swim a couple of laps. The cool

water refreshes me. Then I turn onto my back and float. Floating is more my style than swimming. I look up at the ceiling, which is decorated with a mural of giant red hibiscus flowers, and let myself space out.

I get out of the pool when my fingertips turn pruney. I could go back upstairs and study, but then I think how I deserve to relax a little more. It was a long week at school, especially since I didn't skip any classes. Shouldn't I get credit for that?

I grab my towel and head for the steam room. I'm singing the opening line from 50 Cent's "Candy Shop," swivelling to the beat, when I push open the door.

Only there's someone there. And I think it's Claire Labelle. Maybe it's the hot steam, but for a second, I have trouble breathing. I blink — twice — to make sure I'm not hallucinating.

"Hey Todd, you've got a nice voice," Claire says as if it's the most natural thing in the world for us to run into each other here. Now I know it's her. But I still can't figure out what she's doing here, half-naked in the steam room. Actually, I think she's wearing a leopard bikini, but to be honest, I'm afraid to look. I don't want her to think I'm ogling her.

"What are you doing here?" I ask her. Okay, I admit it's not a very good line, but it kind of pops out. Plus, I am curious. This is the first time I've seen her in the building.

"My grandparents live on the sixth floor,"

Claire says. When she smiles, I notice how white her teeth are. "I try to come for a steam every time I visit. It's good for your pores," she says, turning her head so I can see both sides of her face. Her pores look good to me.

"I'm avoiding Canadian history myself," I tell her.

Claire giggles, and for a second, I feel like the most charming, funny guy in all Montreal. Claire Labelle, the best-looking girl in tenth grade at Hilltop Academy, thinks I'm funny. I suck in my belly and roll back my shoulders, hoping Claire will be impressed. I can't help thinking I should've worked a little harder in our cross-training class.

My heart thumps when Claire pats a spot on the bench next to her. Then I think how now's a perfect time to use my poker skills. I can't let her see she makes me nervous. That would give her a definite advantage over me. So I sail right over and take the spot next to her. We're sitting so close, our knees touch. Claire could move away, but she doesn't. I take that as a good sign.

"So do you live here, or are you visiting *your* grandparents, too?" Claire wants to know.

"We're on the 12th floor."

"In the penthouse?" I think she's impressed.

"What've you been doing all weekend?" I ask Claire. What I really want to know is whether she has a boyfriend.

"Oh you know," Claire says, "studying."

"I wouldn't know."

Claire laughs. I feel myself relax a little more. The steam rises in the air and makes a whooshing sound.

"And I went out," Claire smiles at me, "with my girlfriends."

What I say next comes out so smoothly, so confidently, even I'm impressed.

"How about going out with me next weekend?"

Claire brushes a strand of blonde hair away from her face. "Okay," she says. "Why not?"

I can feel I'm smiling like a madman, so I make myself stop. Hopefully, Claire didn't notice. I need to seem like I'm used to gorgeous babes agreeing to go out with me.

"Why not?" I say, repeating Claire's words. What I'm really thinking is, "Why?"

Claire Labelle has just agreed to go out with me. It's lucky I'm sitting down, because my knees are starting to feel wobbly. Maybe it's the heat. Maybe it's because I'm feeling a little drained. Keeping Claire entertained for five minutes has taken just about everything I've got.

Of course, now I have something way more important than a history exam to worry about. How in the world am I going to come up with a way to impress a girl like Claire Labelle?

Chapter 5

Miss Dodgson is standing at the front of the computer lab, going on about spreadsheets. She's wearing this ruby red miniskirt, so the guys in the class are more focused than usual. No one's passing notes, or staring out the window at the playing field across the street.

I'm sitting in my usual spot at the back of the lab. So I get a perfect view when Larry Johnson, who's sitting up front and has waited for Miss Dodgson to turn her back, winds up his arm like a baseball pitcher and hurls his eraser on the floor.

"Oops," Larry calls out when the eraser lands a quarter inch from Miss Dodgson's feet. The class snickers. We all know what's coming next.

Miss Dodgson leans over to scoop up the eraser. Larry couldn't have done a better pitching job. Because her skirt is so tight, Miss Dodgson has to twist a little at the waist to reach the eraser.

That lets the class see the back of her thong underwear, where the tag is. Hot pink today. Most of the guys' tongues are hanging out of their mouths, like dogs in front of a butcher shop. The girls roll their eyes at each other; they think Miss Dodgson is low rent.

"I think this belongs to you, Larry," Miss Dodgson says, smiling as she hands him the eraser. I notice Larry's fingers are trembling.

There's never a dull day at Hilltop Academy.

"Today we're going to be using spreadsheets for a practical application. I want you people to work on charting a mortgage. Let's say a house costs $150,000," Miss Dodgson says as she walks to the blackboard. The back of her thong has disappeared back under her skirt, but just knowing it's there makes me a little more interested in computer class.

"One hundred and fifty thousand dollars would buy a hovel — not a house," Neil Rutter calls out. Neil lives in a mansion on the other side of the hill in Westmount. A place like that must go for a couple of million, minimum. There's more snickering, but Miss Dodgson is unfazed.

"If our buyer puts twenty per cent down, which is fairly standard, I'd like you to calculate a five-year mortgage at a rate of 4.8 per cent. Then I want you to do the same calculations, but at a rate of 4.4 per cent. Off you go, ladies and gentlemen. By the way, you can work in pairs."

"Who needs a mortgage to buy a house anyhow?" Neil Rutter calls out.

Miss Dodgson looks up from her attendance book.

"When it comes time to buy a house, most people need mortgages," she says a little tensely. "For most people, a house is the single biggest personal investment they will make in their lifetimes," she adds.

"I only ever heard of people paying cash for their houses," Neil explains.

"Or inheriting them," Claire adds, brushing a thick strand of blonde hair away from her eyes.

"We're talking about the real world here. Not just Hilltop Academy," Miss Dodgson says, opening her grade book to show the conversation has ended and we're supposed to get to work.

Lewis is at the computer station next to mine.

"She said $150,000, right?"

"Right," I tell him. "But the buyer puts down twenty per cent."

"Which is $30,000. Which leaves a $120,000 mortgage …" Lewis types something into his computer.

I turn on my computer. Miss Dodgson is still sitting at her desk, making some notes in her attendance book. In a few minutes, she'll start walking around and checking on us, but it'll take her a while to get to our end of the lab.

Lewis has already got a spreadsheet on his monitor and he's talking to himself while he types on the keyboard. "Four-point-eight per cent …"

No use sitting around and doing nothing while

Lewis is working so hard on our assignment, so I visit one of my favourite websites: ugamble.com.

"Have a look at this, Lew," I whisper.

Lewis turns to glance at my computer screen. I've turned off the sound, but the images are totally cool. A deck of huge gold cards, five of them fanned out to make a royal flush. A gleaming stack of poker chips. A twirling roulette wheel. Beautiful women in low-cut dresses. With a little imagination, we could be in Las Vegas instead of the computer lab.

Lewis swats my shoulder. "Aren't you supposed to be helping me here?" he asks.

"I'm helping you, all right," I tell him. "I'm about to perfect my Texas Hold 'em skills."

"Do you think that's a smart thing to do right now?"

"Do you want to spend the rest of your high school years mowing lawns for a living?"

"You'd better turn it off before Miss Dodgson gets here," Lewis says, turning back to his monitor.

"You know how many other people are online right now on this website?" I ask Lewis. A counter has popped up with that information. "Four-thou-sand-nine-hundred-and-thirty-four."

"That many?" Lewis likes numbers almost as much as he likes junk food.

"And I'll bet half of them are bored students."

"Come on, Todd, help me out with the mortgage calculations here, would you?"

I half-listen to Lewis. So far, I've only played

online with what's called "play money." But something tells me I'll be ready for the real thing soon. Especially considering how well things have been going for me lately.

Speaking of which, I take a peek at Claire Labelle. I'm hoping she'll notice, but she's hunched over her computer, hard at work on her spreadsheet. She's wearing the same uniform as the other girls — a grey blazer, white blouse and navy kilt, rolled down at the top — but there's something high-class about her. Could be the perfectly blow-dried, highlighted hair. She's put her purse down on the chair next to her. I know it's a Louis Vuitton, because it's covered with curly Ls and Vs. And knowing Claire, it's not some knock-off from Canal Street in Manhattan.

Claire Labelle is the real thing. I hit the jackpot when I walked into the steam room and found her there.

I type my online name into the computer: 'wannabet.'

A pop-up image asks if I'm ready to play for real money.

I take another look at Claire.

I'm ready all right.

"Turn if off," Lewis hisses. "Miss Dodgson's on her way over."

"Everything all right over here, gentlemen?" Miss Dodgson asks a moment later. By then, I'm standing behind Lewis, peering over his computer screen.

"This exercise really shows how important it is to shop for the best possible mortgage rate. I mean, look at these savings," I say, pointing to the monitor.

When Miss Dodgson smiles, I notice flecks of red lipstick on her front teeth. "Looking good today, Miss," I tell her as she moves on to the next pair of students.

Chapter 6

Olive has Mondays off, so we usually order in. Mom said something this morning about sushi.

By the time I get home from school, I'm too wiped out to do anything except watch TV. We've got one of those new stainless-steel refrigerators with a flat-screen TV on the outside. Which means you can watch TV and snack simultaneously — two of my specialties. I grab some cheese cubes and salsa and start channel-surfing.

Our kitchen reminds me of an operating room. Maybe it's the stainless-steel appliances and the grey and white tile on the floors and walls. Mom calls it "state of the art." Not that she spends much time in the kitchen, except for when she's tearing open the takeout bags.

When the phone rings, I don't bother answering. Whoever it is can leave a message. Besides, I'm just getting into the afternoon game shows.

But when the phone starts ringing again, I figure I'd better pick it up.

"Todd." It's my dad, and though all he's said is my name, I can tell he's stressed out. I hear a fax machine beeping in the background and the sounds of people raising their voices. "I'm sorry, but your mother and I are going to be working late again tonight. We won't be back in time for supper."

"No problem," I say, stretching my legs out in front of me. There are worse things than a night alone in the condo. "I'll grab something from the fridge."

"No," my dad says, "you should order in sushi. Like we planned. In fact, order enough so your mom and I can have the leftovers when we get home."

Sounds like a plan. I'm about to hang up, when I start wondering how he wants me to pay for the takeout. I've only got twenty bucks in my wallet, and sushi has a way of adding up quickly. Especially since I'm planning to order it from Sushi-2-go-go — the new sushi bar on Park Avenue everyone's talking about.

"What do you want me to do for money?" I ask casually.

"Go ahead and use my charge card," my dad tells me. He's never let me use his charge card before.

"You gonna give me the number over the phone?" I ask, getting up from the stool where I've been sitting and crossing over towards the sink. There's pencils and notepaper in the top drawer next to the sink.

My dad pauses for a moment. I figure maybe he doesn't want to give me the credit card number because there are other people in his office. He's not big on trust.

"Bottom drawer, my side of the bed," he tells me. "There's an extra charge card there — under my address book. Use the card. Just make sure to put it back when you're done."

* * *

You have to answer a ton of questions on the poker website before they let you play. Your name, your email address, whether you want your winnings credited to your account, or if you'd rather have them mailed to you, your home address. But there's nothing about your age. They must figure if you're old enough to have a credit card, you're old enough to play for cash. Which suits me fine.

There's a $10 U.S. minimum. I sign up for $50. I figure my dad'll never see the Visa bill anyway. He's got some flunky in his office to take care of stuff like that, probably the same person who schedules his massage appointments and picks up his dry cleaning.

The credit card number alone wouldn't have worked. The website also wants the expiry date and the CVV2 number — that's the last three numbers on the back of the card.

I get my backpack from the front hallway and take out the spiral notebook I use for English. I turn to a fresh page, and copy down the credit card number, the expiry date, and the CVV2. Just in case I need it again.

When I'm back online, I see the familiar royal flush, the roulette wheel, and the hot babes. Only this time, I swear they're smiling at me. One of them has the same colour hair as Claire Labelle.

There's a lot more people online now than there were when I was at school this morning. According to the counter, there are more than ten thousand. Pretty incredible, considering this is just one of hundreds of gambling sites. Sometimes, it feels like the whole world's playing Texas Hold 'em.

There's a long list of poker tables to choose from. There are games where bets start at 25 or 50 cents; others that go up to thousands of dollars. On this site, every table is named after a city: Amsterdam, Turin, Tokyo, Montreal. Montreal is a 25 to 50 cent table. Besides, it's where I live, so I click on it.

The graphics are amazing. My computer screen has turned into a casino. I'm looking at a wooden poker table covered with a green felt top the colour of grass on a baseball field.

One click of the mouse and I'm in the game. There's my online name — Wannabet — hovering over my digital image. On screen, I'm a muscular young guy in a white tank top. The image popped up automatically, but I like it. I look down at my own biceps and make a mental note to work a little harder in gym class.

Three others are already playing when I join in.

Online poker is fast. That's probably because there's less bluffing. The focus is the cards — what you can do with yours, and what the other players might have in their hands. I get dealt a ten and a two, suited. Both diamonds. I feel a surge of excitement that starts in my knees.

Texas Dolly — the greatest poker player who ever lived — won the World Poker Tour championship with a ten and a two. I raise. Two more diamonds come out in the flop. One's an ace.

One of the players — Divine Diva — folds. What are the chances one of my opponents has an ace?

I'm doing some quick calculations when the guy to my left — Cowboy Junkie — folds, too.

A couple of seconds later, the game is mine. I'm up by five bucks. But it's not the money I'm excited about. It's what the money means. And what it means that Claire Labelle wants to go out with me. The thing is, I'm getting used to being a winner.

It's after nine when I log off. I've made a cool fifty bucks, which, according to the website, should be in the mail tomorrow morning. Sure beats mowing lawns.

My stomach makes a rumbling noise. *Christ*, I think to myself as I stand up and reach for the portable phone, *I nearly forgot to order the sushi.*

Chapter 7

It's 11:30, and I'm too wired to sleep.

Every time I try to close my eyes, I see cards. Aces and twos and threes. A jack of spades. I guess I spent too long online.

My parents still aren't home. They must be trying to close some deal. They could at least have phoned to let me know they'd be this late. My body's tired, but my mind feels like a car going way too fast. I keep picturing poker hands, or Claire Labelle in her leopard bikini, or get this, Louis Riel.

Lying in bed definitely isn't working, so I get up and start walking around the condo. My parents' collection of African masks are casting long shadows on the living room walls. "Don't look at me like that!" I say to a particularly ugly one when I pass it.

I walk through the living room towards Mr.

Wonderful's room, at the other end of the condo. I haven't been in there since before he left for Boston. Not that I went in there much when he lived at home. It's not like the two of us have much in common besides the same parents.

When I open the door, the first thing I notice is the smell of furniture polish. Though there's no one around to mess things up, Olive still cleans in here every week. I think she misses Mark. She takes night classes in English, and he used to help her with her homework.

I stop in front of the shelf by the door. There's a whole row of computer books. Windows XP. Visual C++. I look up at the top shelf. That's where Mark keeps his trophies. Lieutenant-Governor's Prize for Mathematics. Hilltop Academy Computer Science Award. Robotics Grand Prize. The trophies shimmer in the moonlight.

Even though we lived in the same house for almost fifteen years, I feel like I'm in a stranger's room. I look around for clues that might help me learn more about my brother. For a second, I'm actually kind of interested.

Mark and me couldn't be more different. Take Mark's desk, for example. Everything's in its place. Pencils — sharpened, of course — in the pencil holder. Pads of notepaper piled up like a pyramid, with the smallest on top.

My own desk is so loaded up with crap, you can't even tell it's made of wood.

I lean over and open the top drawer. A metal

geometry set makes a clattering sound as it slides to the front. Nothing here except a stack of report cards, held together by a thick rubber band. He's got them organized, too, with the most recent on top. No point in looking at them. Who needs to see a row of straight As and the glowing comments that go with them?

Mark is a pleasure to teach. If only I had more students like Mark. We're confident that Mark has a brilliant future ahead. I'm looking forward to teaching Mark's younger brother next year. Of course, that would have turned out to be a disappointment. It's not easy being Mark's brother. Sometimes, I wonder how I would have turned out if I'd been born first.

I'm about to close the drawer, when I notice a laminated card jammed at the back of the drawer. I pry the card loose. It's Mark's driver's license. Guess he figured he wouldn't be needing it at MIT It's not like he goes anywhere besides the library.

But I'll be able to put Mark's license to good use while he's away. I've already got a fake ID a guy at school made me last year, but it looks like a fake. I examine Mark's photo at the top of the license. We may have completely different personalities, but the family resemblance is definitely there. Same dark wavy hair, dark eyes, and the long dark eyelashes everyone says are wasted on a guy.

As my fingers slide along the plasticized surface of the card, I get another idea. I was planning to bring Claire Labelle a bouquet on Saturday night, but I may have just come up with something way more original. Something Claire is really going to like.

* * *

My body doesn't feel tired anymore. Instead, I'm wide awake, energized, ready to roll. I'm back in my room, sitting at the computer. Only now, I'm not gambling online. I've moved my pile of junk over to the far end of the desk. I need room to work.

I just scanned Claire's yearbook picture. Man, that girl is hot. I'd already scanned Mark's driver's license. Now what I have to do is create two separate files and transport the information I need. For a second, I can't help wondering why I can't get this motivated about school.

Shoot. Something's wrong. When I select Claire's photo and drag it over to insert on Mark's ID, the picture of Claire disappears. All I get is Mark — glaring at me like he knows I'm up to no good.

I repeat the operation two times, then a third, even though by then, I know it isn't going to work. I can feel my armpits getting sweaty. "Damned computer," I mutter under my breath. But it isn't really the computer that's annoying me. It's me. Why can't I figure out how to do this thing?

My eyes travel to the top of the computer screen, landing on the word "insert." It's coming back to me now. Something Miss Dodgson taught us in the computer lab. I click on "insert," then I select "picture," "from file," and "float over text." There it is. Claire's yearbook picture. When it appears, I could practically kiss it.

At least now, everything's going according to plan. I type in Claire's name. Next thing I have to do is enter her birth date. The day and the month don't matter — I make it October 2, which is the tenth month and the second day, like Texas Dolly's lucky hand — what matters is the year. I enter 1987, which makes Claire eighteen. Legal in Quebec.

I lean back in my chair and study Claire's picture on the screen. I'd better crop the white school shirt at the top.

I load the printer with a heavy-duty ink cartridge designed for special jobs like the one I'm about to do. Then I remove the ordinary printer paper and replace it with some photo-quality stuff. The printer makes a humming noise when I turn it on.

I watch as Claire's ID pops up. Very nice work, if I say so myself. Then, using an X-ACTO knife, I trim the edges, measuring it against Mark's ID to make sure the size is right.

There's nothing more I can do tonight. I tuck what I've done so far into my spiral notebook. I'm going to be way too tired to go to home room in the morning. When I do get up, the first thing I'll do is stop by the photocopy shop where Lewis's

47

cousin Phil works. I've got a special laminating job I need him to do for me. It's a rush order.

Just then, I hear the key turn in the front door.

"Todd? What are you doing up at this hour, honey?" my mom calls from the hallway.

"Just finishing up a computer assignment for school," I call out.

After she comes in to kiss me good night, I hear her talking to my dad in the kitchen. "You know," she says as she takes plates from the cupboard, "I think Todd may turn out to be just as talented with computers as his brother."

Yeah, right.

Chapter 8

"So you're Todd Lerner." Claire Labelle's dad reaches out to pump my hand. The guy's as big as a bear.

He doesn't invite me in, but from where I'm standing in the front hallway, I get a view of the first floor. There's a huge chandelier hanging in the entrance, thick blue carpeting on the floors leading up a central spiral staircase.

"It's a pleasure to meet you, Todd." I nearly didn't notice Claire's mom. She's standing behind her husband, but because she's only a quarter of his size, she's easy to miss. Claire has her mom's colouring — the same pale skin and blonde-streaked hair.

I resist the urge to shake out my hand after Mr. Labelle's bear grip. Instead, I put it back in my pocket, stretching out my fingers one at a time to help bring them back to life.

"I've come for Claire," I say, trying to sound like I'm used to taking beautiful girls on dates.

"So where are you two off to?" Mr. Labelle asks. He's peering at me in a way that says "Don't mess with my daughter!"

I meet his gaze and give him my best shy smile, lifting my lips just a little at the corners. I want him to think I have nothing to hide, but that I'm slightly intimidated by him. I figure that's what he wants.

"I thought we'd catch the new Batman movie downtown. Maybe go for a walk afterwards," I say, careful not to sound too confident.

Just then, Claire comes rushing down the staircase. She's wearing a blue tie-dyed skirt and a slinky white T-shirt. I try not to notice the way it hugs her chest. Diamond earrings sparkle at her earlobes. She's got a bracelet to match. This chick is one class act.

"Bye Mom, bye Dad," she calls out, waving her hand in the air. "I see you've met Todd." She obviously doesn't want me hanging with the folks.

Mr. Labelle blocks the front door with his body. "Is that a cab you've got waiting outside, young man?" he asks, lifting his eyes towards the street.

"Yes, sir," I say. "I wanted to take your daughter out in style."

"Just make sure you get her home in style, too."

Then he reaches out for another handshake.

* * *

"So we're going to see Batman," Claire says as I hold open the door to the taxi.

"No we're not," I tell her. I turn around to wave at her parents, standing together at the front door. "That's just what I told your dad," I say as I step in behind her.

Claire giggles. She might be a model student, but judging by the giggle, I can tell she likes the idea of putting one over on her parents as much as anyone.

"So where exactly are you taking me, if I may ask?" she asks, smiling up at me.

The taxi driver turns to face me, too. He also wants to know where we're going.

"The casino," I tell them both. The taxi lurches forward.

"We won't get into the casino," Claire whispers. "We're underage."

"What do you mean? You just turned 18." Claire's eyebrows arch in surprise. Then I reach into my back pocket for the ID card I made her. Claire whistles when she sees it.

"How'd you get this?" she wants to know.

"I made it for you. So we could get into the casino. And other cool places."

Claire's eyes widen. "I've never been to the casino."

I don't tell her it's my first time, too.

The Casino de Montréal is on Ile Sainte Hélène, a five-minute drive from downtown. The cab driver mops his forehead when he takes the exit for the casino. There is a long line of cars snaking up ahead, and the exterior parking lots are already full.

"Guess this is where people want to be on a Saturday night," I tell him.

"You kidding?" he says, meeting my eye in the rear-view mirror. "This is where people want to be every day of the week — 24/7."

* * *

"Just show him the card and look cool. Swing your hair or something," I tell Claire once we're out of the cab.

She swings her hair and flashes me a smile. "How did I do?"

In the end, we walk right in. A crowd of tourists are milling at the entrance, noisily exchanging notes about Montreal hot spots. No one cards us. A tired-looking security guard barely gives us a nod.

"He didn't even want to see it," Claire says, sounding a little disappointed as she slips the fake ID card back into her wallet. But then she straightens her back and lifts her head. Even her neck is sexy.

"I feel like I'm 18," she whispers to me.

"You look like you're 18," I say, stealing another peek at her slinky T-shirt.

The first thing we see — and hear — are the slot machines. Even though it wasn't hard to get in, I feel a little rush of excitement now, too. We're suddenly part of this world I'd only seen before on my computer.

There seem to be only old people in this part of the casino, playing for quarters on the slots. I've heard how some gamble away their pension cheques, then live on macaroni and baked beans till the end of the month. The kids at school call them "slot hags."

We're about to step onto the escalator when we hear the wild *ding-dinging* of someone winning. When Claire and I turn around to see where the noise is coming from, we see a blue-haired lady crouched in front of a slot machine, catching quarters in a plastic tub. Around her, other old people begin pulling the cranks on their slot machines more quickly, hoping they'll be as lucky.

"The blackjack tables are upstairs," I tell Claire as we get onto the escalator. Though I haven't been here before, I've studied the layout on the casino website.

Claire is checking the place out. I watch her pale eyes dart from the line of people in front of a cashier's booth, to a red neon sign that says "Montreal smoke meat" over the bar, and then up to the gold panelled ceilings. There are people everywhere, some in glitzy clothes, others wearing sloppy T-shirts and jeans.

"Would you like a Coke or a coffee?" a waitress manning a chrome cart asks when we step off the escalator. "There's no charge," she explains.

"Caffeinated customers must be good for business," I tell Claire. She laughs, and again, I get the feeling I'm the funniest guy on the planet. Another thing I notice is there are hardly any windows — and not a single clock. The idea here is for people to forget about time and the outside world.

I lead Claire to the blackjack tables on the third floor. Hordes of people are crowded around the tables, some playing, some waiting for a spot to open up, and others just watching. We elbow our way through the crowd. The air smells stale, like a mixture of coffee and sweat.

"Let's watch for a bit," I tell Claire. She nods back at me.

We find a spot behind an Asian woman who looks like she's in her thirties. She hands the dealer five $100 dollar bills in exchange for five black chips. Then she stacks the chips on the table in front of her.

I try to imagine her life outside the casino. Where'd she get all that cash? Does she work in an office or own a store, or is she from a wealthy Hong Kong family like Rick's?

The dealer — a serious-looking guy wearing a crisp white tuxedo shirt and black bow tie — deals each player and himself two cards. He only shows one of his cards. A queen, which is a nice start. Claire and I both peek at the Asian woman's cards. She's got a king and a three.

Without looking up at the dealer, the woman

raps her hand on the table — a sign she wants him to hit her with another card. If she's nervous, she's not showing it. Unlike the man next to her, who is tapping the table like it's a drum.

The woman's next card is a jack, so she's over 21 and out of the game. Claire sighs. The tapping guy is still in, only now he's tapping twice as fast. The woman slings her purse over her shoulder, gets up from her stool, and makes a beeline for one of the bank machines that line the wall.

The dealer's over twenty-one, too. All the players still under twenty-one win, including the tapper. The dealer doubles their chips. A casino supervisor strolls by, pausing to watch the action. The dealer pretends not to notice him.

He puts the cards in the automatic shuffler, which makes a whirring sound. Claire and I watch a little longer. I try to keep track of the cards as they come up. Only one ace so far, which means there'll be more soon.

The dealer catches my eye. When the tapper gets up from his spot at the table, I nudge Claire. "Go ahead," I tell her, reaching into my pocket for the wad of cash I brought along to impress her. "Ready to play?"

Claire giggles as I hand the dealer a hundred dollar bill.

"I'll take twenty $5 chips," I tell him.

"Are you sure you can afford to lose all that?" Claire asks, dropping her voice so no one else can hear.

"No problem," I tell her, handing her ten of the red chips. Then I put my ten chips down behind hers. "I'm betting behind you," I explain.

Claire gets a queen and a six. The dealer's showing a jack. "Hmm," I whisper, "it's a bad hand — and a tough call."

"Maybe I should stop," Claire says, her eyes on my face.

"There's always a chance you could get a low card," I tell her. "But I'd say the odds are against you."

Claire's got her hand over her mouth, but I can tell from the corners of her lips that she's smiling. She looks up at the dealer.

"Hit me!" she says.

When she gets a five, Claire throws back her head and laughs. The dealer pulls an eight.

"Twenty-one!" I call out. We just doubled our money.

Chapter 9

An hour later, Claire and I are sitting across from each other at Nuances, the fanciest restaurant at the casino. We could have gone to the all-you-can-eat buffet, the Italian rotisserie, or the deli counter for smoked meat, but none of those would've been good enough for Claire.

I want her to know how much I like her.

There are windows here, huge picture windows that look out over the blue-grey water of the St. Lawrence River. In the distance, we can see the Montreal skyline, and behind that, Mount Royal, the mountain the city was named after.

At first, Claire refused to take her share of our winnings. "There's $100 for you," I said when we cashed out at the blackjack table.

"No way," Claire said, pushing away my hand. "It's yours. I wouldn't feel right taking it."

In the end, I managed to talk her into taking

fifty bucks. "That way I get back the money I staked. You won the rest."

The waiter at Nuances is wearing white gloves, and he's got a linen napkin draped over his arm like a miniature flag.

"Good evening, Madame et Monsieur," he says to us, raising his eyebrows as he hands me the wine list. I get the feeling he knows we're under-age. "Would you care for an aperitif?"

I can tell he's watching my face — waiting to see how I'll react. If I act relaxed, confident, chances are he'll leave us alone. But I've got a lot at stake. What would Claire think of me if we got kicked out of here now?

I take a breath as I turn towards Claire. "How about some wine?" I ask her. I try to sound casual, like I'm used to ordering drinks for girls at fancy restaurants.

"Uh, I don't think so." Claire's face goes pink. Luckily, the waiter's watching me, not her.

"We might have some later — with dinner," I tell him.

"Of course," he says. This time, he smiles.

"My dad'll smell it on my breath when I get home," Claire whispers after the waiter leaves.

"Not if you have two Tic Tacs before you walk in the door."

"Are you trying to corrupt me?"

"Who, me?" I ask, shrugging my shoulders. "No way."

The waiter comes back to pour us water. For a

second, I catch him eyeing Claire, checking out her profile — and her slinky white top. I guess serving beautiful women is one of the perks of his job. Plus, it's got to be good for business to have such a babe in his section.

We order the duck à l'orange. Claire's had it before. I don't even bother to check the price on the menu. After all, I'm a high roller.

"So do you come here a lot?" Claire wants to know.

"You mean to this restaurant?"

"No. To the casino."

"I've come a few times," I lie. Then I reach for the napkin at the side of my plate, unfolding it before I refold it back into a square.

"Tell the truth," Claire says. Her lips pucker like she's trying not to laugh.

It's hard for me to lie when I look into Claire's eyes. They're so blue and so, I dunno, open. They remind me of a lake on a hot day.

"Okay," I admit. "It's my first time here. How'd you know?"

Claire's lips pucker again. I can tell she's having fun. "From the way you were playing with your napkin. I could tell you were nervous."

I let the napkin drop to my lap. Again, Claire's eyes have the same weird effect on me. They make me want to be honest — to stop playing games.

"Maybe that's because *you* make me nervous," I tell her.

"I do?" Claire asks. Suddenly her voice has turned shy.

"You'd make a good poker player."

"I'm not too bad at blackjack, either," Claire says, and we both laugh.

"Want to play again after dinner?" I ask.

"Nah. We should probably quit while we're ahead."

Our duck à l'orange arrives in two silver chafing dishes. When the waiter removes the lids, two puffs of orange-scented smoke drift up into the air.

"We'll each have a glass of sauvignon blanc," I tell the waiter. It's the kind of white wine my dad likes.

A couple of minutes later, the waiter's back with our wine. He nods as he hands me my glass. I hold the glass under my nose and sniff the wine, the way I've seen my dad do.

"Nice bouquet," I say.

Claire smiles.

There are so many knives and forks near my plate, I'm not sure which I'm supposed to use first. I watch Claire for cues. When she picks up the fork and knife that are furthest from her plate, I do the same.

"Playing cards is a rush, isn't it?" I say, as we cut into our duck at the same time.

"Uh huh," Claire says. "Yum. This is good," she adds as she bites into the meat.

"For me, there's nothing else like it," I say. "Well, maybe downhill skiing — when you're taking a really big mogul, and you think you might spill."

Claire nods. I can tell she's thinking about what I just said.

"Aren't you afraid of losing?"

"Nah," I tell her. "Besides, I'm on a winning streak. And like you said, the trick is to quit while you're ahead. What's pathetic is the people who can't quit — even when they're losing."

"Like that lady we saw downstairs. The one who went right to the ATM after she lost all that money."

"Exactly." I take another bite of my duck. I don't want to say anything to Claire, but it tastes just like chicken.

"Don't get me wrong," Claire says. "I like this place ..." She waves her hand around the room so I know she's talking about the restaurant. "But there's something kind of sketchy about the rest of the casino. Everyone feels so ... so ..." She searches for the right word. "Desperate."

I think about the smell of sweat and the old people rushing to the slot machines after the blue-haired woman hit the jackpot.

"I know what you mean. But there's something about gambling that makes me feel really alive. Way more alive than anything else."

"More alive than when you're eating duck à l'orange with me?"

I wonder if I'll have to tell her the truth again this time. "Just as alive," I say, glad my napkin is still in my lap.

I eye the blackjack tables on our way downstairs, but Claire says she'd still like to catch the movie. That way, if her parents ask her if she liked it, she won't have to lie. I figure if we don't have to wait for a cab, we'll make the 9:30 show.

When we're standing outside the casino, a red Audi pulls up at the valet parking. I know it's Rick before he steps out of the car. Thomas is with him.

"Hey man," Rick says when he spots me. Then he turns to Claire. "Whatcha doing with this loser?" he asks, cracking up at his own bad joke.

"Actually, based on our night so far, I'd say Todd's a winner," Claire says.

I could kiss her right then.

Rick turns back to me. I consider popping him one in the face. He must know what I'm thinking, because he claps me on the shoulder and says, "You can take a joke, can't you, man?"

"Enjoy yourselves tonight," I say to him and Thomas. "Just don't go losing all your dough or you won't have any left to lose to me." I figure that makes us even for his calling me a loser.

"Speaking of losing," Rick says, "you coming to my place Friday afternoon?"

Chapter 10

I turn on the TV. There's nothing on but cooking shows. I watch some French chef roll out pastry dough. When I change the channel, an Asian guy and his daughter are making dumplings.

My mom walks into the kitchen, still wearing her housecoat. Without makeup, you can see all the tiny wrinkles around her eyes and over her lips.

"Shouldn't you be studying?" she asks me.

"I'm relaxing," I tell her, keeping my eyes on the TV.

"We never had to remind your brother to study," she mutters under her breath, but loudly enough so I'll hear.

I pretend I didn't hear her. She's only trying to rattle me, and I'm not in the mood to be rattled. I'm still feeling good after my date with Claire. So I try to focus on the dumpling lesson. I watch as the chef shows his daughter how to curl the corners of the dumplings so they look like little pillows.

From the corner of my eye, I notice my mom grab the newspaper from the kitchen counter. I hear the screen door open, and then close when she goes out on the balcony. Hopefully, she'll get so busy with the business section she'll forget all about my study habits and what a disappointment I am compared to Mr. Wonderful.

The screen door opens a few minutes later. This time, my dad walks into the kitchen. "What are your plans for the day, Todd?" he wants to know. His voice is upbeat, but I can tell he and my mom have been talking. She must've sent him back inside to talk to me. Do her dirty work.

"I've got some studying," I say, hoping that'll get him off my case.

"That's good to hear, son. Any chance you'll have some time for a break a little later in the day?"

The question catches me by surprise. I was expecting him to give me a hard time about my study habits.

"What do you mean?" I ask him.

"Well, your mom and I were thinking that maybe the three of us could do something fun together."

Again, I take a few seconds to process what he's just said. We never do anything together. If the two of them aren't working, they're talking about work.

"Don't you have to go into the office?" I ask.

"It's Sunday, Todd."

I consider pointing out how they almost always go in to the office on Sundays. Maybe they've decided to turn over a new leaf or something. Or maybe they're cracking up.

"What were you thinking of doing?" I ask. This time, I look up from the TV.

"We thought maybe we could go for a walk on the mountain."

"Nah," I say, looking back at the TV screen. "I don't think so."

The chef and his daughter have started making dumpling sauce. I watch as she helps him stir together soya sauce and freshly grated ginger. Truth is, even if they have decided to turn over a new leaf and give up their workaholic ways, I wouldn't be caught dead taking a walk on the mountain with my parents in broad daylight. I might as well walk around with a giant L — for loser — on my forehead.

My mom walks back into the kitchen, one section of the newspaper folded under her arm. More and more, I'm getting the feeling they're trying to ambush me. It's like a war, and I'm some innocent villager who was just minding his own business.

"Todd," my mother says, "the three of us need to do more things together."

"Who said?" I ask.

"There's no need to talk to your mother like that," my dad says sharply. What is it with these two? I like them better when they're slaving away at the office.

"It's not like you two have taken much interest in me up to this point," I mutter under my breath. My mom doesn't seem to have heard me. But my dad gets this pinched look on his face.

"Todd!" he says.

I'm wondering if I can get away without apologizing, when my mom suddenly comes up with another idea for a group activity.

"How about we play a board game?"

That's when I laugh out loud. "Mom," I say, turning off the TV, "we never played board games my entire life. Isn't it a little late for that kind of thing now?"

She gives me a pained look.

I slap the side of my head. "Geez," I say, "I don't know how I could have forgotten — but I promised Lewis I'd go over to his house this afternoon. So we can study together."

Five minutes later, I'm in the hallway waiting for the elevator. For no particular reason, I kick the wall. The scuff mark I leave on the wallpaper makes me feel a little better.

* * *

Lewis's dad is in their kitchen, scrubbing his hands like mad under the faucet. He's even heavier than Lewis, which may be why he's breathing so hard. Washing his hands like that is probably the most exercise he's had in months.

"How come your dad does that?" I ask Lewis when I follow him upstairs to the den on the second floor. Lewis gives me a funny look.

"He must've just got off the phone with a client."

"What'd this one do?" I ask. Mr. Stein is a criminal lawyer, which basically means he earns his living defending the scum of the Earth.

Lewis lowers his voice. His little sister Alice is working on the computer, and the door to her room is wide open. He obviously doesn't want her to hear what he's about to tell me.

"This was some woman charged with murdering her kid. I don't know what happened exactly, but it must've been pretty bad for him to be scrubbing his hands like that."

"Guess I'd better be a little nicer to my mom," I say. Only Lewis doesn't laugh.

"What other kinds of sickos has your dad defended lately?" I ask Lewis as we sink into the red corduroy couch in the family room. I rented *Fight Club* on DVD on my way over. Even though I've seen that movie a dozen times, I'm still not tired of it.

"More murderers, a child molester, a couple of bank robbers, and last week, a counterfeiter." Lewis rattles off the list as casually as if he's ordering pizza.

"Doesn't it ever bug you that your dad associates with those kind of low-lifes?"

"Not really." From the irritated look Lewis gives me, I can tell he's lying. "Besides, I hang out with you, don't I?"

Chapter 11

"*To err is human; to forgive, divine.*" Cooper writes the words on the blackboard. When his chalk makes a scraping sound, Anna Browne, who's sitting next to Claire, winces.

"Write that down," Cooper says, turning to face the class. "It's a well-known line; attributed to the British poet Alexander Pope, practically a cliché nowadays." He raises his eyebrows when he says the word cliché. "Although it makes a valuable point about the prevalence of mistakes and the need for forgiveness, it's the punctuation I'd like to focus on today."

That's my cue to tune out. Cooper launches into a discussion about the many uses of the semicolon. I'm wondering if he knows there's an oily stain at the bottom of his blue-striped tie. I wonder if the dry cleaner will be able to get it out. I lean forward to peek at Claire, who's several rows up from me.

She's busy taking notes about the semicolon.

"It can sometimes be used to replace a conjunction like 'and' or 'therefore'," Cooper says. Claire nods as if that's the smartest thing she's ever heard. It occurs to me that if she weren't so hot-looking, Claire might get on my nerves.

Lewis is taking notes, too. When I catch Cooper giving me the hairy eyeball, I open my notebook to a blank page. Tiredly, as if it's taking every ounce of energy I've got, I reach for my pen and make a semicolon on the page. Only then, instead of writing down the other examples Cooper's putting on the board, I turn the semicolon into a spade.

Thinking about cards is way more interesting than punctuation rules.

A minute later, I'm rocking on the back legs of my chair, imagining my future as a professional poker player. I picture myself wearing a slick grey suit, but no tie. I'm striding into Caesar's Palace in Vegas with Claire Labelle on my arm.

"Good evening, Mr. Lerner," the doorman says, practically bowing to the floor as he holds the door open. Everyone turns around to look at us. It's partly because Claire's so beautiful, but mostly because they know I'm a three-time winner at the World Series of Poker.

I pat the thick wad of bills stashed in my front pocket. As Claire and I walk by the slot machines, we pass a thin Asian guy hunched over one of the slots. When he loses, he punches the machine so hard, his wrist starts swelling up. One of the security guys comes over, pats him on the back and tells him it's time to leave.

Claire tugs at my elbow. "Isn't that Rick Lee?" she asks. "He went to Hilltop Academy with us."

I head over to where Rick and the guy from security are standing. From the way Rick is slurring his words, I can tell he's been drinking. It's a habit he picked up at Hilltop after he kept losing to me.

"Rick Lee?" I say, clapping him on the shoulder. "Is that you?"

When Rick starts stammering something about being in Vegas for a toilet convention — it turns out he's in the toilet-seat business — I motion to the security guard that he can go away. "I'll handle this," I say, lowering my voice. Then I reach into my pocket and give Rick a couple of hundred dollar bills. His eyes light up.

"You'd better get back to your hotel room now, old buddy," I tell him. "You need to be in good shape for your toilet convention in the morning."

Rick's hands are shaking when he takes the money from my hand.

"I guess he's fallen on hard times," Claire whispers as she takes my hand. "It was really nice of you to help him out like that."

"Mr. Lerner." It takes a second before I realize Cooper is talking to me. He clears his throat. "What are your thoughts on the subject of regret?"

"Regret?" I ask. "I thought we were doing the semicolon."

71

The class snickers.

"I'm afraid I've digressed since then," Cooper says. "As is my custom."

Cooper is the king of digression, all right. He can hardly stay on the same subject for five minutes straight. He's always coming up with some observation — the people he's noticed in line at the drugstore he goes to, the way some people organize their clotheslines from smallest to biggest, that kind of random stuff.

If you ask me, regret is a depressing subject, but still, it's way more interesting than semicolons.

"They say we're supposed to live so we don't have any regrets," I say. I watch Cooper's face for his reaction. I'm hoping he'll back off now and ask for someone else's opinion.

But Cooper's not done with me yet.

"They?" he says, raising his eyebrows. That's when I realize he's about to get even with me for not paying attention. Cooper's like that.

"They," I say, repeating the word. "As in most people — the general public."

"Are you saying," Cooper asks, looking straight at me, so that for a second, it feels like there are just the two of us in the room, "that you tend to be in agreement with the opinions held by most people — by the general public?"

"Well, I guess …" I'm stumbling about for what to say next when Lewis pokes my elbow. When I turn to look at him, I realize he's trying to tell me something. His lips stretch out like a line, then they purse together again. My mind's racing to try to figure out what Lewis means and then suddenly — eureka! — I get it: "Cli-ché."

"It's a cliché," I say. "That thing people say about living life so we won't have any regrets — it's a total cliché." Cooper is obsessed with clichés. He thinks they should be banished from the English language. This'll make him as happy as a snow day in February.

"That's perfectly right," Cooper says, and I feel the muscles in my stomach relax. It's bad enough to have to sit through classes all day, but it's even worse when a teacher singles you out and starts asking you questions.

"In fact," Cooper continues, "I was reading a fascinating new study about regret." Way to go. He's going to start yakking all over again — which means I can tune out for another five, maybe ten minutes.

I straighten my back, and then I do this thing with my eyes — open them extra wide to make it look like I'm concentrating. Next time, Cooper looks at me, I'll throw in a nod. Let him think I'm really into his latest digression.

On the outside, I'm looking keen. But on the inside, I'm getting ready to tune out. Relax. Contemplate my life. But there's something about Cooper's voice — an urgency that makes me think he's really interested in what he's saying. So I keep listening.

"Research indicates that regret may actually have value. It can lead us to make important changes in our lives. The study also shows that North Americans' number-one regret —" he stops to emphasize the words *number one* "— involves education. Either that they did not remain in school long enough, or they did not work hard enough when they were there."

Once he says that, Cooper's eyes travel around the room, landing just for a second on the slackers, which include me, of course.

I lean back in my chair, tilting my head so I can see the puffy white clouds through the window behind me.

"The thing I regret about school, Sir," I say, "is having to show up."

When the class cracks up, I join in. Cooper's smiling, but his lips are pulled tight. I can tell he's bluffing.

"Hey Todd," Claire says after the bell goes and we're walking out of class. For a second, I don't realize she's talking to me. I'm too busy thinking about regret.

Chapter 12

"I'm not sure it's a good idea."

"Sure it is." Lewis can get very stubborn sometimes. We're walking past the Mount Royal Cemetery on our way over to Rick's. This time, Lewis wants to play poker. I'm just not sure he's ready yet.

"What's a flush?" I quiz him.

"Five cards of the same suit. A Royal Flush is even better. It's an ace, king, queen, jack, and ten — suited."

Leave it to Lewis to come up with that extra information about the Royal Flush. What does he think he's going to get — bonus points?

What worries me is, when it comes to poker, knowing the rules isn't enough. You've got to be able to read people, and that's not something you can get from a rule book or the *Poker for Dummies* DVD Lewis bought at Blockbuster last week.

Just as we're walking up Rick's front stairs, a silver Mercedes pulls up next to Rick's Audi. A small Chinese woman with her hair pinned up in a bun steps out of the passenger seat. She must be Rick's mom. When she walks, she takes tiny, deliberate steps.

When the driver gets out, I know right away he's Rick's brother. He's got the same tall, skinny build and round shoulders.

The woman stretches out her hand to shake mine and Lewis's. Her diamond ring catches the light. There are even chunks of diamond floating inside the face of her watch. She's obviously loaded.

She says something else. I think it's "Good afternoon, gentlemen," but it's hard to know for sure because of her thick Chinese accent and the way she nods her head when she talks.

"Nice to meet you," I say, shaking her hand and moving into impress-the-parents mode. "This is Lewis."

"We're here to play poker with Rick and his buddies," Lewis blurts out.

I glare at him, but Lewis doesn't seem to notice. So much for his straight A average.

Rick's brother, who's been unloading dry cleaning from the trunk of the Mercedes, walks over to the side of the car where we're standing.

"We just got back from the casino ourselves," he announces.

* * *

Mrs. Lee is upstairs taking a nap. Lawrence, Rick's brother, is in the basement watching TV. I can hear the laugh track from some sitcom. When Lawrence joins in, his laugh, which is really loud, comes out like a hee-haw. It's got to be the dumbest laugh I've ever heard. You can tell he has no idea we can hear him from upstairs. I try not to let it distract me.

The same two guys that were over last time are here again. The dealer button is in front of Thomas, so he's shuffling the deck.

"Don't you think it's a little strange — your brother going to the casino with your mom?" Lewis asks Rick.

"It's no big deal," Rick says. "For us, gambling's a family activity. When I was a kid growing up in Hong Kong, I played mah-jong with my grandmother. For money."

We all laugh.

"Did you beat her?" I ask Rick.

"Mostly, but sometimes I let her win."

When Lewis checks his cards, he practically turns them over for everyone to see. I've told him a million times to just lift one corner. I shake my head.

"Hey," Thomas says, "no secret signals."

"That wasn't a secret signal. I just don't want him to be an idiot."

Lewis blushes, but after that at least he lays his cards flat on the table.

I've got a three-eight offsuit. Not so promising. Still, I raise the bet to $10 when it's my turn. I lean back in my chair and try to look relaxed.

Lewis, who's next to me, calls my raise. I can feel him watching my face for my reaction. I'd nod — just to make him feel better — but I don't want Thomas freaking out on me.

Rick wins the first hand. Lewis and I are both down forty bucks. When Rick grins at me, I try to remember how he looked in my daydream — punching the slot machine till his wrist was swollen.

* * *

Believe it or not, Lewis wins the next three hands. I'm still behind, but losing to Lewis feels way better than losing to Rick.

When I glance at Lewis, I can tell he's trying to swallow a smile. He's definitely got to work on his poker face.

It's my turn to deal. When I peek at my cards, pocket queens, I start feeling hopeful again. Of course, I make sure not to let that show on my face. Instead, I chew on the inside of my cheek — making sure the others notice me doing it.

Everyone folds except for Rick and me. I'm in for $20.

I bite the inside of my cheek again when I see the flop: there's a king, a four — and another queen. Things are looking pretty sweet for me now.

Rick raises by $10.

"I'll re-raise by $20," I say, keeping my eyes glued on Rick. That's when he reaches for his sunglasses and puts them on. Aha! That's a sure sign he's got something to hide. But what are the chances he's got pocket kings? Not too high. No, I can feel it in my bones, this is going to be my big win. The win that's going to make up for the rest of the afternoon.

"I call your bet," Rick says, sliding another $20 worth of chips into the pot. The corners of his lips turn up, but the look he gives me is more like a sneer than a smile.

It's time for the turn. I burn one card and turn over the next one. Six of spades. Not very interesting.

"I'm gonna raise you again," Rick says, putting another $20 into the pot. This time when I look at him, he turns away. That's when I decide he's bluffing.

"I'll re-raise you another $20," I tell him.

Gimme a queen, I say to myself when it's time for the river — the last community card. Since my fingertips are already under my chair where no one can see them, I let them grip the upholstered bottom. I'm starting to feel a little anxious. The thing is not to let it show.

Gimme a queen. But no, when I turn this one over, it's a king.

Rats!

"I'll raise you by $30," Rick says. His voice is cool, unrattled. Could he have kings after all?

"I'll call your $30," I say. I can feel my heart thumping hard inside my chest. If I lose now, I'm down $120. Add that to my earlier losses and I'll be down over $200.

I feel my breath catch in my throat when Rick shows his cards. He's got three kings, and for a second, I could swear one of them is winking at me.

"Trip kings," Rick says, laughing. "Can't beat that now, can you?"

I make a point of not looking at Lewis. The last thing I want now is sympathy. Rick is saying something about how he has to leave for dinner with his mom and brother at some fancy restaurant downtown, but I'm listening to another voice.

It's a quiet, nervous voice and it's coming from inside my own head. *Hey man*, it's asking, *what if your winning streak is over?*

Chapter 13

Things start looking up the next morning when Claire phones. She wants to know if I'll go shopping with her downtown. What Claire doesn't realize yet is I'd do just about anything she wanted me to.

"I thought you told me you don't usually phone guys," I say when we meet up at the bus stop on Park Avenue.

"I don't." Claire blushes and for a second, I feel guilty for embarrassing her. "Usually."

It's one of the warmest days so far this spring, and even though I'm not into flowers, I notice some little yellow ones popping out from under a fence.

"So where we going?" I ask her when we find two seats together at the back of the bus.

"I thought we'd start out at Les Cours," Claire says. She means Les Cours Mont-Royal, this mall near Peel and Ste. Catherine Streets. My dad told me there used to be a hotel there when he was growing up. "It's got all my favourite shops. Luscious. Deluxe and American Babe. I saw a great pair of capris at Luscious. They're blue-black, kind of like the night sky in summer."

Claire gets a dreamy look in her eyes when she talks about clothing.

I nod my head and try to say "uh-huh" in all the right places. I know capris are a kind of pant, but otherwise, Claire is talking a foreign language. For the first time ever, I wish I had a sister who could give me a crash course in girls' shopping habits. We could call it Malling 101. Or in my case, Remedial Malling.

Claire and I end up transferring onto the métro and taking it to Eatons Centre. From there, you can take the underground walkway over to Les Cours.

Claire makes her way easily through the thick crowd of Saturday shoppers. She holds her head high, and her eyes are focused on some spot I can't make out, but which I suspect must be her favourite store. The one with the capris in it. I've practically got to jog to keep up with her.

Our first stop is Luscious. The salesgirl — a brunette with legs so long they belong on a horse — is busy with another customer. Claire heads straight for a rack of clothes at the side of the store. She sorts through the rack like it's pages in a phonebook, a look of total concentration on her face.

"They're gone," she says, covering her mouth with one hand. You'd think someone had died.

I'm not quite sure what to do. Offer my condolences? I'd feel funny sorting through women's clothing, but I get the feeling Claire needs help. Her face is flushed and I'm wondering if she's about to have some kind of meltdown. I shift from one foot to the other, then move a little closer to the rack and start searching. "You said they're navy blue, right? Size four?"

Claire looks up at me. "Blue-black," she says.

"Is this them?" I unhook a hanger from the rack and hold up a pair of dark pants that look like they were designed for an amputee.

"Oh my God," Claire squeals. "You found them! You're amazing!"

When we're standing at the cash, I'm so close to Claire I can smell the lemony scent of her shampoo. I lean in for a kiss.

Claire takes a step back and laughs. "Maybe later." Then she rubs the end of my nose with her index finger. My knees get a little weak. What is it about Claire that she can make touching a guy's nose seem sexy?

"You're cute," she says. "Not to mention a very good shopper."

* * *

An hour later and I'm starting to feel like a mule. For one thing, I'm carrying four bags. One's got shoes in it. Claire is trying to explain the psychology of shopping to me.

"The way it works is," she says, tilting her head back when she laughs, "you get one thing — like the capri pants — and then you realize your shoes are totally wrong." Claire looks down at the canvas sneakers she's wearing. They look fine to me. "You need a new top. And then your purse doesn't work with the shoes."

"It's an addiction," Claire sighs when we're on the escalator, heading up to the next floor.

"Does that mean you start shaking or sweating when the stores close at 5 p.m.?" I make my arm, which is resting on the escalator railing, start trembling. Then I wipe my forehead with my other hand. Claire giggles. See, she does think I'm funny.

Truth is, I'm starting to wonder how much more of this shopping expedition I can take. I've spent most of the day waiting outside dressing rooms while Claire makes oohing and aahing sounds.

But then I catch our reflection in one of the mirrors lining the walls near the escalators, and I think how lucky I am to be spending the day with a babe like Claire. Other guys would kill to be carrying her bags — or standing outside her dressing room.

Our next stop is a small boutique selling jewellery and sunglasses.

"I love these ones," Claire says when she tries on a pair of sunglasses. They're made of white plastic, but because they're Chanel, they cost four hundred bucks.

Claire's already spent over $500 — not that I'm keeping track. She told me how her parents let her go on a shopping spree at the beginning of each month.

"Imagine how much more it would cost them if I didn't go to a school where we have to wear uniforms," she says.

"I don't know if I should buy them." Claire has taken off the glasses, and now she's holding them in her hands like they're a newborn baby. "They're gorgeous," she coos, running her fingers along the shiny white plastic. "But way too expensive."

Claire puts the sunglasses back on the glass shelf where she found them. When we leave the store, she turns back for a second and sighs.

"Hey," I say, digging my hand into my back pocket, "I think I might've dropped my bus pass in there."

Back in the store, I pretend to be checking the floor. But I really went back to talk to the salesgirl.

"I'd like a business card, please," I say.

As soon as my game picks up, I'm gonna buy Claire those sunglasses.

Chapter 14

I pick up the phone to call Claire, but then I put it back down. With a girl like her, I need to play my cards right. I can't seem too eager. Too cool isn't good either.

I lie back down on my bed. I try to tune out, listen to some music on my iPod, but I keep thinking about Claire.

I got that kiss she promised me — but not at Les Cours, or even on the bus ride home. No, Claire held out till the very last second. We were standing at her front door. Except for the front light, the rest of the house was dark. Even so, I had the feeling her dad was lurking behind some curtain, keeping an eye on us.

I was planning how to move in for the kiss, when Claire surprised me by reaching for my hand, pulling me towards her, and kissing me on the lips.

I have to admit I was pretty surprised. But I got over it quickly. Her lips felt soft, kind of like rose petals, and I could tell from the way they were pressing down on mine that I could take things a little further. So I let the tip of my tongue find its way into her mouth. For a couple of seconds there, it was like I was in heaven.

I was just thinking how Claire was even hotter than I ever imagined, when I felt her palm pressing against my chest. The insides of my stomach quivered. Only then, she pushed me away.

"Sorry," I muttered. "I guess I got carried away."

"Me too," Claire said, a little breathlessly.

The whole way home I kept replaying the way Claire had said, "Me too." There was no question about it. Claire Labelle had the hots for me.

I knew I'm decent-looking, I knew I had a pretty good sense of humour. But that was the first time I realized that I, Todd Lerner, might just be a babe-magnet.

* * *

"It's Mark on the phone!" my mother calls from the living room. From the way she says it, you'd think the Messiah just landed in Montreal. "Stephen, it's Mark!"

I hear my dad opening the door to his den.

"I'll be right there!" He sounds as excited as she does.

I try to tune them out, but it's hard because they're on the speakerphone and its crackling echo carries all the way to my room.

"Oh that's wonderful!" my mom says. I put a pillow over my bed, but even that doesn't drown out her gushing.

"Amazing!" my dad says.

Mr. Wonderful must be boasting about his latest grades. They must've known something when they called him Mark; the guy is obsessed with marks. I turn over onto my side and turn up the volume on my iPod.

All this reminds me of how I did on the history quiz. Forty-two per cent — pretty good if you consider I didn't study for it. At least my parents forgot to ask how it went.

"We're so proud of you!" my dad says. I wonder if he's deliberately trying to annoy me.

"Todd!" my mother calls out. "It's your brother on the phone." As if I hadn't figured that out. "Don't you want to speak to him?"

I make a groaning sound as I drag myself up from my bed and head for the living room. I figure if I move slowly enough, Mark might hang up before I get there. No such luck.

My mother pats the spot on the sofa next to her. "Todd's here now, too," she announces. "He wants to talk to you." Yeah, right.

"How ya' doin'?" I ask. I try to make it sound like I care.

"I'm doing great," Mark says. Not a surprise,

since Mark is always doing great. "I was just telling Mom and Dad how I aced my mid-terms. And my computer engineering prof wants to hire me this summer to be his research assistant. It's a tremendous honour for a first-year student."

I'm thinking, if Mark is so smart, why doesn't he realize what a self-centred jackass he sounds like? If I don't cut him off now, he'll keep rattling off his list of accomplishments. I'm sure there are more.

I suck in my breath. "I'm really proud of you," I say.

For a second, there's dead air on the other side of the phone. I catch my mom and dad exchanging a look. You can tell they think I've finally made progress in my relationship with my brother.

"You are?" Mark asks.

"Sure thing. You're an amazing guy ..." I can practically hear Mark smiling on the other end of the phone. "... for a dork."

* * *

"That's no way to talk to your brother," my father tells me after Mark hangs up. He's wagging his finger in the air like I'm some puppy who refuses to be paper-trained. Which in a way, I guess I am.

"Let him be," I hear my mother say when I get up from the couch and head back to my room. Then she lowers her voice. "Having a brother like Mark can't be easy."

* * *

I want to go back to thinking about Claire, but I'm too jumpy.

So I turn on the computer and scroll down my list of favourites until I get to the poker site.

Once I'm online, I start feeling better. I reach into my backpack for my spiral notebook. I'm going to be needing my dad's credit card information again.

"*That's no way to talk to your brother*," I mutter, mimicking my dad. Then I enter the CVV2 number.

The computer asks how much I want to deposit into my poker account. I'd been thinking $300, but then I remember those Chanel sunglasses. My finger moves to the right on the keyboard — $600 — that sounds about right.

Chapter 15

Two things can happen when you play poker online: you can win big or lose slowly. So slowly, you don't even notice you're losing.

Which is what happens to me.

I start by scrolling past the 25 cent tables. Today, I've set my sights a little higher. Besides, I've got $600 to play with — and I'm hoping to buy Claire those sunglasses with my winnings.

Last time I played online, the $50 I won turned up in the mail three days later in an unmarked white envelope. Which means I should be able to go back to Les Cours after school on Wednesday afternoon for the sunglasses. I can practically see the look on Claire's face when I give them to her.

Those sunglasses will be my way of letting Claire know how I feel about her. The thought makes me move my chair a little closer to the computer.

This time, when I click on an empty spot at the virtual poker table, my pop-up image isn't some muscular guy in a white tank top. Instead, I'm this little old lady with a face that looks like a shrivelled potato. There's an ugly black purse and a wooden cane on the floor by my — I should say her — feet.

The bets at this table start at $10. My first two cards are a pair of nines. Nice start, I think, as my body moves right into poker mode: my eyes focus on the screen and I feel my heart starting to race.

I raise the big blind's $20 to $30. I want my opponents to know I'm serious. There's a six, a queen, and a nine in the flop.

When I spot the nine, I have to stop myself from slapping my knee. For a second, I forget I'm playing online and that my opponents can't see or hear me any more than I can see or hear them.

"Yes-ss!" I call out. Not having to hide my feelings feels good — like getting out of school at the end of a long boring day.

"Everything okay in there?" my dad's voice asks. I'm so into the game, I forgot where I was.

"Uh ... sure," I say, hoping he'll go away. I hope I'm not gonna have to shut down the computer, not when things are looking so good.

"Wanna watch a little basketball with me?" my dad asks.

"How about later?" I say, without lifting my eyes from the screen. I try not to sound like I'm trying to get rid of him. I don't need him thinking I've got something to hide.

"Okay," my dad answers. Then I hear him head back down the corridor to his den.

I was sure those trip nines would win me the hand, but some guy named Wildchild beats me with trip jacks. Crap.

A little black-and-white box at the bottom of the screen tells me how much money's in my account. I'm down $40, but hey, it's no big deal. I've still got $560 to play with. Still, I wish I could shake the feeling that things aren't going my way. Part of me is starting to feel like some shrivelled old lady who should be knitting or napping — not playing poker.

I could log off, maybe watch some hoops with my dad, but that'd be quitting too soon. The action's just getting started. I probably just need a little time to warm up and get into the game. Any minute now things are gonna change for me, I can feel it.

My confidence starts to come back when I win the next hand. *Yes!* I think to myself as I see my account's back up to $590. My neck and shoulders relax.

They tense up again when I see my cards. A three and a six. Usually, I'd wait for the flop before folding, but this time I go ahead and fold. It's like I'm spooked. I moan out loud when a three and a six turn up in the turn and the river. I mean what were the chances? Two pairs would've given me the hand. But instead of feeling disappointed, I decide to take it as a sign. It's time to play more aggressively.

The thing is: you need to think like a winner when you play poker. I've seen it happen a million times. A guy thinks like a loser and he loses big-time. Think like a winner, and everything goes your way. I should try my theory on Cooper. Maybe he could find a way of working it into one of his lectures.

I'm up a little, then back down, like a thermometer that's not working right. For a while, my account hovers between $500 and $700. I don't stop to check what time it is because I'm concentrating so hard on the cards. I don't know if I've been playing for fifteen minutes or two hours.

A few more hands and I'm down again — this time to $450. My hole cards are a king and a five. *Gimme another king*, I whisper when the flop comes down. But there's no king, not even a five. This time, I don't fold. No, I'm gonna bluff. It's all a matter of confidence, right? If I act confident, I'll win. Isn't that all there is to it?

Only, it turns out, if your opponents have bad cards. Beautyqueen, a big-busted blonde who just joined our table, has a pair of aces. She wins the hand and I'm down even more.

I've stopped thinking about Claire's sunglasses. All I can think about now is recovering my losses. My next hand is bound to be better. A guy can't just keep losing like this. Or can he?

My hands get a little sweaty when I drop below $400, then below $350. I wipe them on the front of my jeans and shake out my shoulders. Anything to change my luck. I could stop now, but I'm convinced that if I play a little longer, I'll win back what I lost.

I hear my dad's footsteps outside my room. I want to tell him to go away, to leave me alone, but of course, I don't. The footsteps stop, but then a few seconds later, I hear them again. Is he back in his den? In the distance, I hear the sounds of the basketball game: cheers and the drone of an announcer's voice.

Just a few more hands, I tell myself. It's my turn to deal, which gives me an advantage, since I'm the last one to bet. I've got a jack and a king, suited. For the first time in a while, I start feeling hopeful again.

"As long as you have hope, you have life," I can hear Cooper say. "Except for false hope. False hope can be a dangerous thing."

I bring my hands to my ears to block out Cooper's voice. I need to concentrate on the cards. There's a ten and an ace in the flop. All I need now to make my straight is a queen. This time, I check. There's nothing for me in the turn. Two of my opponents fold. I feel that surge of hope again — there's still the river, and though I can't see my opponents, I can almost feel their tension. Are their hands sweaty, too?

I hold my breath as I wait for the river. The computer makes a clicking noise as the card is revealed. An eight.

But I can still bluff. I raise to $100. Beautyqueen isn't giving up. Either she's bluffing, too, or she has the winning hand. She raises to $200. Now I can feel my armpits start to get sweaty. I click on the raise icon. If I lose now, there'll be nothing left in my account.

If I win, Claire'll be wearing those sunglasses on Wednesday afternoon. We show our cards. Beautyqueen has trip eights. As for me, I've got nothing. And neither does Claire.

Chapter 16

I'm only pretending to watch the basketball game. My dad's got his arm looped over my shoulder and my mom just brought us a bowl of microwave popcorn. Part of my mind registers there's a game on — it's the L.A. Lakers versus the New York Knicks — but mostly, I'm numb. The popcorn has no smell, I can't feel the touch of my father's fingers when he traces a small circle on my sleeve, and the sound coming from the TV is just a noisy whir.

I've lost my touch. Not to mention my dad's six hundred bucks. My hands and feet feel cold, and there's a pit at the bottom of my stomach. How did I lose the money so fast, anyway? And why didn't I stop myself before the account was empty?

It's a stupid question, of course. If it weren't for my dad's arm, which has me pinned to the couch, I'd be back at the computer, at another poker table, trying to win back the money. Trying to win more money. It's that shrivelled-up old lady's fault. She jinxed me; I know she did. If I'd been that cool guy in the white T-shirt, I'd have won. Won big.

"There's no way in hell he travelled!" my dad shouts, jumping up from the couch so suddenly, that for a second, the hardwood floor vibrates.

"Can you guys pipe down?" my mom calls from the hallway, where she's checking messages on the answering machine. Some workers are coming to remodel one of the bathrooms starting tomorrow, and she's waiting to hear what time they're supposed to get here.

"Goddamn referee," my dad mutters. "He's giving L.A. the ball."

"For goodness sake, boys, it's only a game," my mom says.

I try to concentrate on the game. The score is tied at 84 and they're in the final quarter. I know I shouldn't go back online anyhow — at least not now. I'm feeling too desperate. Better to wait till later, when I'm calmer.

I feel a little guilty when I look at my dad. It's his money after all. Not that he'll notice. Still, I'll win it back, I know I will. And when I do, I'll get the site to credit his charge card.

He's back on the couch, his fingers gripping the dark leather. I can tell that if he could, he'd pounce on the referee.

"Marbury was dribbling — not travelling!" my dad insists.

"Uh-huh," I say, though the truth is, I wasn't watching when the ref made his call. I look up at the TV screen and tell myself to think about basketball, not poker.

I'm watching the screen when Marbury, the New York point guard, turns to the ref. Marbury's face is red, sweat's dripping down his cheeks, and he's making a fist with one of his hands. I can't hear him, but from the way his lips are moving, I'm pretty sure he's saying something like, "What do you mean? That's bull!"

The camera zooms in on the ref. He doesn't look too happy to be talked to like that. My dad's laughing out loud. So loud he has to lay his hand on his stomach to make himself stop.

"Glad to hear you boys are having fun!" my mom calls out. Then she closes the den door so she can continue listening to her messages. No one's surprised when the referee calls a technical foul.

"If you want my opinion, the ref had it coming," my dad says.

The Lakers' coach calls his players over to the bench. They're about to get a free throw. After that, they get possession of the ball.

"This is some game!" my dad says, punching my arm.

There are only three seconds left in the final quarter. If L.A. sinks this shot, they'll probably win the game.

A lanky guy with curly blond hair steps forward to take the shot. I watch as he crosses to the shooting line and eyes the net. I figure he's doing what they tell us to do in gym: visualizing success. Maybe he's imagining the swishing sound the ball will make when it sinks into the hoop.

"I'll bet you five bucks he misses the shot," my dad whispers.

I suck in my breath. In all my 15 years, my dad has never once made a bet with me.

"You wanna bet?" I ask him.

"Sure," my dad says, as if it's the most natural thing in the world. "Five bucks says he misses."

The L.A. shooter is bending his knees to prepare for the shot. He's holding the bottom of the ball with one hand, and using the other hand to guide it towards the hoop. He has to be six-foot-five, at least.

"I'll bet you ten he makes the shot," I say, careful to keep my voice cool, level. I don't want my dad to know I'm excited — that my heart has begun to race, the way it does whenever I make a bet.

"Ten it is," my dad whispers, without lifting his eyes from the TV.

I always liked watching basketball, but now that I've got money riding on the game, I have a whole new interest.

Neither of us says a word as the ball flies out of the shooter's hands, making an arc in the air before it begins to drop just a little. First it skims the side of the rim, then it bounces up and hits the backboard, and then it hits the other side of the rim, circling to the left. For a second, it looks like the ball's about to drop to the ground, but then, just like that, it sinks into the net.

"I won!" I say, and for a second, everything in my life feels better.

My dad reaches into his pocket and takes out his wallet. He peels a ten-dollar bill from his wad of bills.

"If I were you," he says, dropping his voice, "I wouldn't mention any of this to your mother."

Chapter 17

"Why didn't you tell me we had an English quiz?" I whisper to Lewis as Cooper hands out the question sheets.

Lewis looks around to make sure Cooper isn't watching us. I don't know why he's so nervous. We don't even have the quiz yet. "I tried, but your mom said something about you and your dad bonding."

"I bet him ten bucks the L.A. shooter would get that last basket."

"You made a bet with your dad?" For a second, Lewis forgets to whisper.

"Are you two gentlemen at the back having a problem?" Cooper asks, staring at us over the edge of his wire-rimmed glasses.

"No, sir," Lewis says, straightening up.

"You can turn the test sheets over now," Cooper says.

As I turn mine over, I get a glimpse of Claire's blonde hair. Like usual, she's up at the front. For a second, I wish I'd paid more attention in class. I wish I could ace this test, just to impress her.

Cooper wants us to interpret this poem about a sunflower. I have a hazy memory of talking about it in class. "Why does William Blake use an exclamation mark between the words 'Ah' and 'Sunflower' in the poem's title?" Beats me. But leave it to Cooper to come up with a question that involves punctuation. I bet he wishes that Blake dude had thrown in a semicolon too. That would've really made Cooper's day.

I put my pen down on the desk and make a sighing sound. Loud enough for Cooper to hear. Then I lift the palm of my hand to my forehead. My head feels warm and clammy. Excellent.

When I feel Cooper's eyes on me, I wince. Cooper's a decent guy. I'm banking on the fact he won't leave me here to suffer during his quiz. Three seconds later, he's hovering over my desk like a mother hen.

"Feeling all right, Mr. Lerner?" he asks.

Things are going even better than I planned. There are worry lines on Cooper's forehead. If I were a nicer guy, I might actually feel sorry for him.

I pick up my pen — to show him I really want to write the quiz. But then I let it fall out of my fingers so it looks like I'm too weak to hold it.

After that, I make my final move. Subtle, but

deadly. I bite my lower lip. "I'm not feeling too well," I whisper.

The others are already scribbling away on their answer sheets. Cooper bends down so his head is at the same level as mine.

"You sure this doesn't have anything to do with our quiz, Mr. Lerner?"

I look straight at him. "Of course not, Sir."

"In that case, I'd like you to go down to the nurse's office. Have yourself checked out. You'll write the quiz tomorrow during lunch. If you're well enough."

"Thanks," I mutter, gathering up my things from the floor. I'm careful not to rush out of the classroom. I don't want Cooper thinking I've recovered. When I open the classroom door, Cooper is looking at my answer sheet. I don't know why he's bothering. All it's got on it is my name.

* * *

"Don't tell me you've come down with another fever, Todd," Mrs. Browne says when I knock on her door. She's been working as the nurse at Hilltop since I started here way back in kindergarten.

"It just hit me out of nowhere."

"Let me guess. Did it strike during an exam or a class presentation?" She reaches into her top drawer. That's where she keeps the thermometer.

"I hope you wash that thing," I tell her as I sit down in the chair next to her desk.

"Say 'Ahh!'" Mrs. Browne says as she pops the thermometer into my mouth. From the corner of my eye, I take a peek at the brass lamp on her desk. If she leaves her office, the way she sometimes does — to get a message or talk to the headmaster — I could hold the thermometer over the bulb and arrange to give myself a light temperature. It's an old trick, but it's worked for me before.

But Mrs. Browne doesn't have any messages and the phone doesn't ring. When the thermometer makes a beeping sound, she takes it out of my mouth. Then she holds it to the light to read it.

"Thirty-seven degrees centigrade," she says triumphantly.

"It's my head," I tell her and I bring my palms to my forehead, like I did in class. "It's throbbing."

Mrs. Browne gets up from her chair and walks over to the medicine cabinet on the wall across from her desk. She reaches in for a bottle of Tylenol. "Have two of these with a little water. You can go back to class next period — after whatever it is you were avoiding is done."

There's a knock on Mrs. Browne's door.

"There must be something going around," I tell her.

But it's not another sick kid — or a kid pretending to be sick. It's Lewis.

"I came to check on him once I finished the English quiz," he tells Mrs. Browne, lifting his eyes in my direction.

"Ahh," Mrs. Browne says, "an English quiz." She looks Lewis up and down, stopping at the bulge where his stomach hangs over his pants. "Are you trying to cut back on the calories, the way we discussed?" Lewis's face goes red. If he hadn't come to check on me, he wouldn't have had to put up with Mrs. Browne's weight-loss tips. Any second now and she'll be discussing vitamins. Then, like clockwork, she lifts her head to look at us. "Are you two taking your multi-vites?" she asks.

* * *

"He'll never give you the same test tomorrow," Lewis tells me as we walk down the hall to the computer lab for our next class.

"I know," I say, "but at least I'll be able to study for it tonight."

"Did you really make a bet with your dad last night — or were you kidding about that?" Lewis wants to know.

"I only bet him ten bucks." I don't know why Lewis is getting so excited.

"Sports betting's huge," he says, his voice kind of breathless. "Guys make thousands doing it."

I look at Lewis and grin. I can't believe I never thought of it before. Sure, I've heard guys talk about betting on sports, but for some reason, I never thought about doing it. Too busy with Texas Hold 'em, I guess. This could be a whole new venue for me. Suddenly I notice I'm getting the old adrenaline surge.

"Or lose thousands," Lewis adds. Only by then, I'm not really paying attention.

Chapter 18

"We're beginning our unit on web page design," Miss Dodgson announces as we file into the computer lab. "But today, I'd like you to work alone," she adds.

I can tell the guys are disappointed. Not just that we won't be working in pairs, but also because Miss Dodgson is wearing a long skirt with a baggy pink blouse. Why would someone with a body like Miss Dodgson's dress like your grandma?

Miss Dodgson clears her throat. "As I mentioned last class, I wanted you to give some thought to a possible subject for your personal web page. Since you people will be working on your pages for the next two to three weeks, I recommend you come up with topics that will maintain your interest for that period of time."

I honestly have no memory of Miss Dodgson telling us to think up a topic. The funny thing, though, is I can tell you exactly what she was wearing last class: a navy blue dress with white polka dots. The neck was so low-cut, I decided not to take my usual bathroom break during class.

Truth is there isn't much that interests me. Besides gambling.

That's it! The perfect topic — one I'd never lose interest in.

"I'd like you to begin by doing some preliminary research," Miss Dodgson calls from the front of the lab, "to see whether similar websites already exist." She writes the words "Preliminary Research" on the board.

For the first time since we studied dinosaurs in Grade 2, I'm actually kind of excited. The computer makes a dinging sound when I turn it on.

"I'm handing out a sheet on which I'd ask you to report on the topic you've chosen — and your progress so far," Miss Dodgson says.

When Lewis hands me the sheet, I take it without looking at him.

"What're you working on?" he asks, but I'm too busy to answer.

I write the word "gambling" in the space Miss Dodgson has left blank for the topic. Next, she wants a list of five related websites we've consulted. I don't even have to look up the first one. It's on my list of favourites on my computer at school: ugamble.com.

When I Google the term "sports + betting," I can't believe the number of hits I get. Hundreds. I can't be bothered going through them, so I copy the addresses of the first four. There, all done.

Miss Dodgson smiles when she walks up to my work station. I've filled out the sheet and laid it on the corner of my desk where she can see it. She's probably not used to me being a model student.

Miss Dodgson picks up the sheet. The polish on one of her nails is chipped. I watch her face as she scans the sheet. Maybe she'll make me change topics.

But then she smiles again. "Nice start, Todd. However, I think your topic needs some narrowing down. For instance, you might want to create a web page with tips to help prevent gambling addiction in young people."

I might.

Or I might not.

* * *

When I think about it later, I realize Miss Dodgson was on to something when she mentioned tips. Only I'm not interested in tips to help stop kids from gambling; I'm interested in tips to help them win. Now that's the kind of web site I'd be interested in. Once I get it up and running, I shouldn't have trouble finding sponsors — big companies like Coca-Cola or Telus. In fact, chances are companies like that will hear about my web site and come to me. Offer me all kinds of money to advertise on my site.

I'm starting to imagine combining my career as a professional poker player with running the website. That'd be seriously cool.

Instead of leaving the building when school ends, I do something I've never done before. I stick around to do some extra work. Besides, it'll be noisy at home now that the workers have begun renovating the bathroom. For what I'm planning to do next, I'll need to be able to concentrate.

There are a couple of other kids in the computer lab. Geeky types. I give one of them a quick nod, then head for the computer I was using during Miss Dodgson's class.

Just doing my research, I tell myself as I log onto a sports betting page.

This time of year, you can bet on hockey and basketball. I click on basketball. Tonight, the Lakers are playing the Miami Heat. According to the information on the screen, Miami is favoured to win at minus-five. Which means if I bet on Miami, they have to win by at least five points, which is pretty close considering how high the scores get in basketball. If I bet on the Lakers, they've got to win, or lose by less than five.

I picture the lanky blond Laker who won the game for them last night — and earned me ten bucks. *Yes*, I think to myself, *the Lakers can do it*.

My spiral notebook is open on my desk. I flip to the page at the back where I wrote down my dad's credit-card information.

It looks like I'm about to open another account.

* * *

It turns out you don't have to wait to activate your account on this website. They're going to let me make a bet right away. I feel little sparks of electricity shooting through my arms and legs.

The computer is asking how much I want to bet on the Lakers. First I type in $100. I look at the three digits on the screen. They don't look like much. I hesitate for a few seconds and then, just like that, I type in another zero. Now that's a bet. If the Lakers win, I'll be up $1,000. That'll clear up my debt to my dad and pay for Claire's sunglasses.

After that, maybe I'll take a bit of a break from gambling. Maybe I'll concentrate on school. Just to see what it feels like.

Who am I kidding? That little voice inside my head is back. It's telling me I'm in too deep to stop.

Chapter 19

The game starts at eight. That gives me forty-five minutes to study for the poetry quiz. I stretch out on my bed, propping the pillows under my head. It takes me a while to get comfortable, but once I am, I start reading over the sunflower poem. Once, twice. Even then, I don't exactly get it. I could keep reading, but instead I pick up the phone and call Lewis.

"Why did Blake put an exclamation mark after the word 'Ah,' anyway?" I ask him.

Lewis must be eating. I can hear him making crunching sounds on the other end of the line.

"I told you, Todd," he says between crunches. "There's no way in the world Mr. Cooper'll give you the same questions he gave us."

"I just want to know why, is all."

Lewis sighs. He must've finished his chocolate bar.

"An exclamation mark indicates strong emotion or surprise," he says. You can tell he memorized that line from his notes. Lewis would never use a word like "indicate." "The poem's a deeply emotional poem."

"But what's it about?"

"Cooper says it's about time and reaching for something higher. You know, the way sunflowers grow — it's like they're reaching for the sky."

"Uh-huh," I say, scribbling down what he's said in my notebook. I still don't get it. I mean, who cares about a flower's feelings? Maybe if I write down what Lewis says, it'll sink in later. Like a basketball sinking in the net.

Lewis seems to be reading my thoughts. "So you watching basketball tonight?" he asks me.

"Uh-huh. In fact, I've got money riding on the game," I say casually.

"What'd you do? Make another bet with your dad?"

"Nah, I logged on to one of those sports betting sites you were talking about. It was part of my web page research for Miss Dodgson. Those sites are pretty cool, Lew. If L.A. wins tonight, I'm gonna be up ..." I pause for dramatic effect, "one thousand big ones."

Lewis makes a gulping sound on the other end of the phone. "One thousand? You're kidding, right?"

"Why would I kid you? So Lew, I'm nearly done studying the poem. Why don't you come over and catch the game over here? I've got good snacks."

"I can't." Lewis sounds disappointed. "I promised I'd help Alice with her homework. I'll probably just get to watch the final quarter. Only, after what you just told me, I'm not sure I can handle the stress."

After I hang up, I read the poem two more times. In between, I check my watch. Only twenty-three seconds have gone by since the last time I looked. Maybe I'm as obsessed with time as the sunflower. Only I can't figure out what the "something higher" is I'm supposed to be reaching for.

* * *

When, five minutes later, the phone rings, I know before I pick it up that it's my dad — and I even know what he's going to tell me. They won't be home in time for dinner. There's plenty to eat in the fridge. Go ahead and help yourself. If we're not back too late, we'll pop into your room to say good night. Your mom and I are awfully sorry, Todd. We promise we'll make it up to you.

"It's a shame you won't be around to catch the game," I tell my father before I hang up.

"Don't tell me you were planning to make another ten bucks off of me," he says. I can hear him chuckling as he puts down the phone.

I chuckle, too. After all, what's ten bucks to a high roller like me?

* * *

I should be studying the poem some more, but sometimes, it's really hard to do what you're supposed to. I keep getting distracted. I keep checking my watch, and now I've started daydreaming about what I'll do with my winnings. I could buy myself something — maybe some new CDs. The funny thing, though, is there's nothing I really want.

I can download music from the Net, and it's not like I'm into clothes — or sunglasses. Which makes me realize that, for me, gambling isn't about winning money so I can buy myself stuff. Yeah sure, I want to have money so I can spoil Claire — buy her stuff and take her out to fancy places. But I guess, for me, gambling's mostly about winning. Maybe that's my something higher.

* * *

I turn off the game at the end of the third quarter and let the remote fall to the floor. When it hits the hardwood, one of the batteries pops out and rolls across the room, landing under a wing chair that once belonged to my grandfather. I don't bother picking the remote up.

When I turned off the game, the score was 48 to 12. For Miami. One of their shooters scored the opening points from the free throw line. I don't think I've ever seen such sloppy work or more fouls from the Lakers. What's wrong with them?

There's no way in the world they can come back now — and I can't take watching anymore. It's too painful. My hands and feet are cold, and I can feel my body starting to shiver. Maybe the air-conditioning is on too low. Maybe I'm getting sick — for real, this time.

Why didn't I bet on Miami? They were favoured to win, after all. If I'd bet on them, all my troubles would be over. I'd be able to clear up my debts, buy Claire those sunglasses and give them to her this weekend.

But no, I went ahead and bet on the Lakers, and now I've lost $1,000. I try to make the thought go away, but it won't go. Somehow, it feels like all this is happening to someone else. Like I'm floating somewhere and looking down at this guy shivering on a couch. The guy's a loser. The guy's lost his touch. The guy's winning streak is oh so over.

The guy is me.

When the phone rings fifteen minutes later, I'm still sitting on the couch with my hands on my thighs, staring up at the ceiling.

This time, I know it's Lewis. He must've caught the end of the game. I'll bet he's phoning to offer his condolences — and tell me I should never have put money on the game. I don't bother picking up.

Chapter 20

"You're still looking a little peaked today, Mr. Lerner," Cooper says when I walk into his classroom at 12:05. "The nurse assured me that whatever ailment you were suffering from yesterday wasn't life-threatening."

I never heard the word "peaked" before, but I figure it probably means tired. Which I definitely am. Just thinking about how tired I feel makes me start yawning. I cover my mouth so Cooper won't give me a hard time. He's got this thing about students not covering their mouths when they yawn. Only he calls our mouths "yappers."

Last night had to be my worst night ever. I started feeling nauseous about all the money I'd lost. Every time I thought about it — or how pissed-off my parents were going to be if they found out — I felt like I was going to puke. I had this awful taste in my mouth: sour, bitter. But I was too miserable to get up from my bed and bring my garbage can over in case I really did throw up. So I just lay there, staring up at the ceiling like a zombie. How could I have screwed up so bad?

My parents have been upset with me before — about report cards and what they call my "insufficient effort" at school. But something like this would drive them right over the edge.

I kept thinking how things would have been totally different if only I'd bet on Miami. If only! I even imagined myself back in front of the computer, feeling all revved up. But in my imagination, I bet everything on Miami. When I wasn't thinking about all that, I started worrying about how I wasn't getting enough sleep. Plus I couldn't get comfortable in bed. My pillows felt lumpy and the sheets made my skin itch.

Cooper sits at his desk at the front of the room while I write the quiz. He's eaten his sandwich and now he's clipping his fingernails. Isn't that the kind of thing you're supposed to do in private? I mean, if you're fussy about people covering their yappers when they yawn, wouldn't you also have rules about where they clip their fingernails?

Lewis was right about Cooper coming up with a new question: "How are we human beings like the sunflower?" The weird thing is, I think I might actually know the answer this time. Maybe it's because I'm so tired.

In the poem, the sunflower is "weary of time," which is exactly how I'm feeling right now. So I write a paragraph about how people get tired of doing the same kinds of stuff all the time — getting up in the morning, rushing out to school, doing homework, then getting up the next day and starting all over again — and how they get tired of worrying about things that are going wrong, and also tired because they haven't been getting enough sleep.

In my second paragraph, I write the stuff Lewis told me — about how the sunflower is reaching for something higher.

"Like we human beings …" I know you're supposed to use the teacher's words when you answer a test question "… the sunflower wants to find someplace better to go. Even though he's just a flower, the sunflower seems to be searching for some kind of high. Don't get me wrong, I don't mean booze or drugs or anything like that. What I mean is that the sunflower doesn't want to spend all his time thinking about rain and whether there are enough nutrients in the earth to feed him. He wants to do something that'll make him feel amazing. That'll lift him out of his daily routine, out of the earth."

I have the feeling I did a good job on the answer — even if I didn't manage to find a spot where I could use a semicolon.

Cooper looks up when he notices me shuffling in my seat. "Allow time to read over your work," he says, peering at me over his glasses.

If he hadn't said so, I'd never have bothered reading my test over. Mostly, I just want to meet up with my friends in the caf. But when I read my answer over, I suddenly realize something. When I was describing the sunflower's feelings and how he wants to reach for something higher, I was talking about me — and how I feel when I gamble.

I'd always thought poetry was for losers — for guys with pimples who can't get dates, or for girls who've got no friends and stay home and study all weekend. But when I hand in my answer sheet, I can't help thinking how maybe I was wrong.

* * *

When I walk into the caf, Claire is milling around the table where I usually sit.

"You waiting for me?" I ask, sliding my thumbs through the two front belt loops on my pants.

Claire blushes. "N-no. Not really. I just wanted to know if you're feeling better. And if your makeup test went okay."

"The test actually went fine. And yeah, I'm feeling better. A little tired is all. Thanks for asking." I'm about to ask Claire if she has plans for the weekend, when my cell phone starts doing a little dance in my pocket. I've got it on vibrate.

At first, I don't recognize the number on the screen. It's my parents' office number, except for the last digit, which is a seven instead of a five.

"I should probably see who this is," I say, looking back up at Claire.

"Hey, Claire," a voice calls from behind us at

the same time I start speaking into the phone. In the background, I can hear Rick talking to Claire: "A few of us are going over to Costa's for iced tea," he's saying. "Wanna come?"

"Is this Todd Lerner?" a strange voice asks.

"Uh-huh, yes, it is." For a second, I wonder if something's wrong with my parents.

"Are you calling from my parents' office?" I ask.

"As a matter of fact, I am. My name is Edgar Milne. I'm your father's assistant. I need to talk to you about some unusual charges that appear on your father's latest credit card statement. I thought it might be wise to talk to you before I speak with your father."

I take a deep breath. Just when I thought nothing else could go wrong, this jerk phones me up. In the distance, I can see Claire walking out of the cafeteria with Rick. When he tries to put his arm around her, she shakes it off.

I pick at the food on my plate. Today is veggie burgers, but because I got to the cafeteria late, mine is cold.

"Look," I say, lowering my voice so the other guys at my table won't hear, "maybe I should go somewhere where I can have a bit more privacy." I expect Edgar Milne to say something, but he doesn't. So I get up from the table and head for the hallway. Luckily, it's deserted.

"What's going on e-exactly?" I ask. I try to sound cool, but my voice is shaky and my face feels hot.

Mr. Milne clears his throat before he starts speaking again. "I phoned Visa about an unexpected charge to Mr. Lerner's, I should say, your father's, account. They were able to trace the charge to a gambling operation in upstate New York and they told me you were the originator of the charge."

"Are you sure it's not a mistake?"

"I'm quite sure. I also learned that another charge went through last night. That makes a total of $1,600. I don't think your father will be very pleased when I tell him what's going on."

"Do you really have to tell him?" My voice comes out sounding squeaky.

"Monitoring invoices is part of my job."

From the way he's talking, you'd think he was the freaking minister of finance. There must be something I can say to talk him out of ratting me out.

"Wait! What if I could pay the company back — by next week? With interest even, if that'll help."

Mr. Milne doesn't say a word. I take that as a good sign. He must be thinking about my offer.

"The truth is, Todd," he says at last, "your father has a lot on his mind without having to deal with your ..." He stops to find the right word. "Transgression."

"Just give me a week."

"There'll be no need for interest. If you can clear this situation up within a week's time, I don't think I'd feel obliged to share the details with your father." Mr. Milne pauses and when he speaks again, his voice sounds sharper. "But if you can't repay the company within a week, don't think I'm going to jeopardize my own situation by covering for you."

"I understand," I tell him.

"There is one other thing …"

"What is it?" I ask. The whole time my mind is going full-speed, trying to come up with ways to raise the money. I have to get back online.

"Unless you're ordering takeout food, there are to be no further charges on your father's account. Absolutely none. Are we agreed on that, Todd?"

Chapter 21

On Wednesdays and Fridays, there's an activity period after lunch. Sometimes, there's a guest lecturer — like this woman in a hijab, a political scientist, who came to talk to us about the Middle East. If there isn't a lecture, students who are in clubs or on student council have their meetings. Other kids use the time for homework, or if they're like me, to hang out and do as little as possible.

Today though, I'm actually considering going back to the computer lab to work on my web page. Except that this week, being around computers is stressing me out. It's because I know if I just had access to a credit card, I'd be able to win some cash online and clear up my debt.

I talked to Lewis about getting me his parents' credit card number, but you'd think from the way he reacted I'd asked him to take a flying leap off the Champlain Bridge. "There's a lot of stuff I'd do for you, Todd, but not that," he said. I could tell there wasn't any point trying to convince him otherwise.

What I need to do now is think. I figure a good place to do that would be my great grandfather's bench. That's this wrought-iron bench he donated to the school. It's got his name on it, engraved on a brass plaque. It's under this weeping willow tree at the edge of the playing field.

I've got to come up with a way to make money. I can tell I'm in bad shape from the weird ideas going through my head. Like just now, I was actually trying to calculate how many lawns I'd have to mow to raise $1,600. Way too many.

As I'm walking down the front steps, headed for the playing field, Rick sidles up next to me.

"Hey man," he says, "if you're not doing anything special, why don't you come to chess club?"

"Chess club?" I repeat. "You gotta be kidding. Chess club's for nerds."

"You calling me a nerd, man?"

"Uh-huh, that's exactly what I'm calling you." Giving Rick a hard time is helping take my mind off my troubles.

Rick takes another step down so we're both on the same level. He's so close now that when he speaks, I can feel his warm breath in my ear. "Chess club is just a front," he whispers.

"A front? What are you talking about?" I ask, but my mind is already figuring out the answer. Could it be what I think? And if it is, has the solution to my troubles magically appeared — like a row of cherries on a slot machine?

Only then, it hits me that things aren't quite so simple. For one thing, I'm broke. Totally broke.

"I thought a bright boy like you would be able to figure out what really goes on at chess club," Rick says, nudging my elbow.

I really don't want to tell Rick about my little problem. That would give him a psychological edge, which is what you really don't want to have happen when you play poker. I make a mental note to include that tip on my website. Do whatever you can to avoid showing any signs of weakness to your opponent.

But I'm in a special category: I don't have a choice.

"Listen, Rick," I say, in a voice that makes it sound like we're old buddies. "I'd love to come to uh … chess club, but the thing is …" Here I hesitate a little to let Rick know that what I'm about to tell him is privileged information, and that I'm only telling him because we're so close. "I'm a little short on cash."

There. I've said it. It's out. I haven't told him how short, of course.

"Not to worry, man," Rick says, clapping my shoulder. "The Rick Lee Bank would be happy to extend you a little credit. At a reasonable interest rate, of course."

I really wish I didn't have to take Rick up on his offer.

"What kind of interest rate were you thinking

of?" I ask. "Not that I'm planning to lose."

That cracks Rick up. "Who plans to lose?" He laughs some more, then clears his throat. "Twenty-five per cent — monthly," he says. I could say how that's way more than even the credit card companies charge, but I decide not to. Besides, I can tell from Rick's voice that he means business.

* * *

Chess club meets in Room 205. Near the door, two seventh-graders are playing chess, leaning over their boards, pondering their next moves. But, as Rick explains, that's not all they're doing. They're on watch — keeping an eye out for teachers who wouldn't be too happy if they knew what was going on at the back of the room.

That's where four guys are huddled around a chessboard. From the way the pieces are positioned, you'd think there was a game going on, with two of the guys playing and the other two watching. But the chessboard's just for decoration — like a vase of flowers on a table. There's a game going on, only it's not chess.

I get the familiar buzz as soon as I sit down. We're playing tournament-style poker — which means you buy in up front — for $200. Rick hands me the cash under the table so no one else'll notice.

My first two hands aren't promising, so I fold. I'm minimizing my losses, which is a good strategy for a guy in my position. My next hands are stronger. My mood improves as my pile of chips begins to grow. Now it's the other guys who are folding.

Within fifteen minutes, I'm up over $600. *Yes*! I think to myself. *This is it.*

My next hand is a queen and a ten. Nice start. I don't react when a queen doesn't appear in the turn or the flop. When it's my turn to bet, I raise. One guy folds, then another, and then another, until it's just me and Rick, head to head.

When he raises, I raise again. It's like he's teasing me. I should be more careful, but I can't seem to stop myself from continuing to bet. Not now.

"I'm all in," I say, pushing my pile of chips towards the mountain near the chessboard.

It's time for the river. Finally, a queen! Rick bites his lip. It looks like he didn't get whatever he was waiting for.

I can feel my heart thumping as I show my cards. "Pair of queens," I say, hoping that'll be enough to win.

Rick winces. That must mean I've won, right?

"Pair of queens," he says, turning over his cards. "But my kicker's higher than yours." My other card was a ten; Rick's got a jack.

One of the seventh-graders has left his post at the door to watch our game.

"Rick wins the pot!" he calls out.

As if I hadn't figured that out.

Chapter 22

"You *what?*" Lewis throws his arms up into the air. "Are you nuts?"

"You don't have to shout," I tell him. My nerves are shot. All night, I worried about the money I owed. Even when I finally fell asleep, my mind seemed to stay awake, adding up my debts like a calculator that wouldn't turn off — $1,600 to Mr. Milne; $875 to Rick, which includes the twenty-five per cent interest.

"Look, I know it was dumb. Really dumb. But the thing is, I've got to come up with a solution. Fast. But Lew, are you sure you can't get me the credit card number?"

Lewis's face goes red.

"Okay, fine," I say, "forget I mentioned it."

Lewis's face goes back to its normal colour, but he's still breathing kind of heavily.

"I feel bad for you, Todd, really I do." Then he

reaches into his drawer for a sheet of paper. "Let's brainstorm. See if we can come up with any ideas."

I'm so desperate I don't say what I'm thinking. That brainstorming is for school assignments, not life.

Lewis runs a chubby finger along the skin between his nose and mouth. "Is there any way you can just talk to your parents? Tell them what happened, and get them to pay off your —"

"No way," I say, cutting Lewis off. "Just imagine how good this mess'll make Mr. Wonderful look."

Lewis nods. He knows all about my brother.

"What about a job?" Lewis asks, jotting the word "job" down on the sheet of paper.

"There's no way I can earn that kind of money — not quickly anyway," I tell him.

"We've got to think outside the box."

"Lewis! Lewis! I need you!" It's Alice, calling from her bedroom down the hall.

Lewis looks at me apologetically. "Sorry," he says. "Sounds like another arithmetic crisis. Do you mind?"

"No problem," I tell him, taking the sheet of paper from his hands. "I'll work on this. Go ahead. Don't worry about me."

"Okay, I'm coming!" Lewis shouts, picking himself up from the corner of his bed where he's been sitting. As he leaves his room, I notice how slumped his shoulders are.

A minute or two later, I can hear the steady drone of Lewis's voice as he tries to explain the arithmetic problem: "If x is greater than y, and…" I look down at the list and cross out the word "job." I write the words "MAKE MONEY," and then I write the word "HOW" with a big question mark next to it. There must be some way to make money.

I spend the next few minutes staring at the sheet. Nothing comes to me. Part of me wants to crumple it up. Part of me still hopes Lewis and I will be able to come up with something. But it sounds like Lewis is going to be busy for a while. I start fidgeting in my chair, rocking on the back feet.

I'm way too anxious to sit still. So I get up and walk around Lewis's room for a bit, stopping to peer into his garbage can, which is filled with candy bar wrappers. But somehow, I feel trapped in Lewis's room. Like an animal in a cage. I need more room. I need to move, stretch my legs. Maybe that'll help me think.

Lewis doesn't notice when I walk by Alice's room. But Alice does. I point at the math homework on her desk, and she rolls her eyes.

I head downstairs. Usually, the door to Lewis's dad's study is closed, but today it's half-open. I stop to see if anyone's inside, but the room is empty. Mr. Stein has this cool contraption that looks like a guillotine by the window. When we were in elementary school, Lewis told me how it was really an antique candle-snuffer. Not that that ever stopped us from pretending it was a guillotine.

For a second, I wonder what it'd be like to have your head chopped off. They say chickens keep walking around for a while after they're decapitated, but of course, it wouldn't work the same for people. As I'm thinking these creepy thoughts, I gradually make my way into Mr. Stein's office. He's got this old red leather chair where he sits. It's probably an antique, too. The leather on the armrests is worn.

I nearly jump when I hear a low buzzing sound. Is there an alarm in here? But no, I realize quickly the sound is coming from under a file folder on Mr. Stein's desk. He's left his BlackBerry — it's a gizmo that's like a combination minicomputer and telephone — and now it's ringing.

As quietly as I can, I leave the room. Though the BlackBerry only made a low ring, Lewis and his sister still might've heard it. It wouldn't look good if they found me in their dad's office. Especially considering the kinds of cases he handles.

That's when the idea occurs to me. Make money. Some people specialize in *making* money. What was the name of that counterfeiter Mr. Stein defended, anyway? The guy's name was all over the newspaper. I wrack my brains trying to remember.

Come on, I think to myself. This is way more important than remembering names and dates for some history quiz. And then, just like that, the counterfeiter's name comes to me: Kevin Weaver.

From the sounds of it, I can tell Lewis is still helping Alice. So I go back into the office and over to Mr. Stein's desk. Only this time, I reach for the BlackBerry. I wonder if I'll need a password to get into the personal files. But no, Mr. Stein has left it on. He probably had to leave the house in a hurry and forgot the BlackBerry.

I scroll down the menu until I get to a file called "Address Book."

The rest is easy. Kevin Weaver's phone number is exactly where it should be — under the Ws. I reach for some paper from the note block on Mr. Stein's desk and take down the number.

Before I go, I try to make sure everything is in its place. I line the note block up at a right angle to the blotter, put back the gold pen I used to write down Weaver's number. I slip the BlackBerry back under the file folder. But now I can't remember whether Mr. Stein's chair was tucked into the desk. Could I have moved it when I was reaching for the BlackBerry? I remember thinking how the leather on the armrests looked worn. So it couldn't have been tucked in. When I slip out of the office, my heart's pounding. I leave the door half-open, just like I found it.

The telephone rings. This time, it's the land line.

I can hear Alice picking it up in her room.

"Hi Dad!" she says. "Hold on," she adds a moment later, "I'll go down and see if it's there."

Only then she gets a better idea.

"Todd!" she calls out. "Are you downstairs? Can you do me a favour and check to see if my dad left his BlackBerry on his office desk?"

I have to swallow my laughter. You've got to admit, it's kind of ironic, Alice asking me to check on her dad's BlackBerry. I guess I shouldn't have bothered worrying about whether I'd moved his chair.

I'm careful not to answer straight away. Instead, I walk back to Mr. Stein's office and open the door completely so it makes a creaking sound. Then I take a little longer to rummage around on the desk. Finally, I reach under the file folder.

"It's here!" I call back upstairs.

Lucky for me, I'm good at bluffing.

Chapter 23

"Waddya say your name was?"

"Todd Lerner. Like I told you, I need to meet with you. I'd like to buy …" I stumble for a minute as I try to come up with the right words. "Some of what you sell."

"How'd ya get my number?"

"I, uh, can't really say."

"Why should I even keep talking to you?"

I'm afraid he's going to hang up — and then I'll really be screwed. So I figure I might as well tell the truth. I don't have anything left to lose.

"Look," I tell him, "I'm in Grade 10 and I'm in a little trouble."

When Kevin Weaver laughs, it comes out like a long, slow cackle.

"What school do you go to, kid?" he asks when he finally stops laughing.

"Hilltop Academy."

Kevin Weaver whistles. "That's some fancy school. Whaddya say your name was again?"

"Lerner. Todd Lerner."

"I see. Any relation to the rich Lerners? The ones in Outremont? Manufacturers, aren't they?"

"Yup," I say, hoping maybe that'll keep him from hanging up. "My great grandfather founded Lerner Mills. My parents run the company now."

He whistles again, and then for a couple of seconds, he's silent, so I figure he must be thinking.

"Todd," he says at last, sounding a little friendlier. "As you can probably understand, with the trial going on, a guy like me needs to keep what they call 'a low profile.' But I'm gonna do something for you, because you sound like a decent guy — and because you're from a decent family. The kind of family that'll back you up if things go wrong. I'm gonna give you the name of one of my, uh, associates."

* * *

The associate's name is Patrick — it turns out there are no last names in the counterfeiting business, not unless you get caught and your name turns up in the paper like Kevin Weaver's.

Patrick doesn't look much older than me. I meet him outside a bar on de Maisonneuve Blvd. in Montreal's east end. Except for a stud in his chin, and his hair, which looks like it needs a good combing, he seems like a regular guy.

"Let's go for a little walk," Patrick says, looking over his shoulder to make sure no one's following us. "What's that monkey suit you're wearing?" he asks, turning to eye my blazer.

"School uniform," I tell him. Suddenly, I wish I'd gone home after school and changed into jeans.

"Oh, right. Weaver told me you go to some fancy-ass school at the top of the hill."

As we turn the corner, Patrick pulls a twenty-dollar bill from his pocket and hands it to me. "Is this one of the ones you made?" I whisper as I take it from him.

"Yup," Patrick says. "Pretty nice, isn't it?"

I rub the green bill between my fingers. It feels crisp, like a regular new bill. I study the Queen's face, the wrinkles over her lips, her pearl necklace. Then I inspect the hologram that runs along the left side of the bill. I've heard that part's hard to get right. I turn it over and check the other side. It looks fine to me.

"Show me some more," I say. After all, the guy could be trying to pull one over on me. How do I know he didn't just show me a real bill, and now he's going to try and sell me a stack of duds?

But the other bills look just as good. Patrick's not too happy when I tell him I can't pay him up front. He wants $5 for every one of his twenties.

"I'll give you six — but I need a week before I can pay you," I tell him.

Patrick studies my face.

"Ever play Texas Hold 'em?" I ask.

"Sure," he says. "I don't know if you've noticed, but the whole world's playing Texas Hold 'em these days."

"What I'm trying to tell you is I'm not bluffing. I'll have the money for you …" I stop to check my watch. It's five to six. "By this time next Friday."

"Weaver told me who your dad is." Patrick says it slowly, like I'm supposed to know he's sending me another message besides the actual words. "If you don't pay up on time, I'll be talking to Pops."

It's a threat, of course. But I don't get upset. I understand that, like me, Patrick's just doing what he has to do. I offer him my hand. "It's a deal," I tell him.

* * *

If you think it's hard to sell counterfeit money, you're wrong. In fact, after the first afternoon, I didn't even have to look for customers. They came looking for me. Mostly, I sell to seventh-graders. They're all a bit afraid of guys my age, so I have an advantage over them.

"If you rat me out," I tell each of the kids I sell the phony money to, "you'll be in big trouble. And I mean *big*." None of them asks what I mean by that, so I don't need to elaborate. But a couple of them turn pale on the spot, and another one's hands actually start shaking like he has that disease old people get.

"Look," I told him, "there's nothing to worry about. Just forget you ever met me, okay?"

Poor kid could barely get out the word "okay."

I sell the twenties for $12 apiece. That's a 100 per cent mark-up — just like in the stores. (See, I learned something in economics last year.)

"I'll take ten of them," this kid with curly black hair and pale blue eyes tells me when he meets me in the parking lot behind Hilltop.

"That's a hundred and twenty bucks. In tens," I add. I don't want any twenties because I don't want them paying me off with my own fake bills. The kid holds one of my twenties up to the light, the way they do in stores when they're checking for counterfeits.

"What I don't get," I say as I count the pile of ten dollar bills he gives me, "is where you guys in seventh grade get all the cash. When I was your age, I was living on twenty bucks a week allowance."

When he laughs, he throws his head back. "Twenty bucks? You gotta be kidding. I get a hundred a week. But I have to pay for my own movies," he says as if that explains everything.

After recess, Lewis is lurking near my locker.

"I saw you talking to some little kid outside," he says accusingly. "You hanging out with seventh-graders now?"

"You got a problem with that?"

"No. As long as you're not selling them dope."

"You don't exactly have a lot of confidence in me, do you?" I ask Lewis.

140

"So what were the two of you talking about?" he wants to know.

I look right into Lewis's eyes. "I was giving him some tips — about adjusting to high school."

"Yeah right," he says, rolling his eyes.

Truth is, spoiled thirteen-year-olds make good clients. The kid with the curly black hair tells one of his friends, who tells one of his friends. By Tuesday morning, I'm nearly sold out.

It isn't until I'm holding the last three twenties in my hand that I notice something strange. I don't know why I didn't think of checking this out before. The last three bills all have the exact same serial number: AZP3771444.

I try not to worry. Hey, if I didn't notice it till now, why would anyone else?

Chapter 24

I decide to give myself the afternoon off. I've been under a lot of pressure lately, so I figure I deserve it. Besides, I've got lots to do. I start by writing my note for tomorrow. I take a piece of my mom's stationery from the kitchen drawer and produce what I consider to be an excellent imitation of her handwriting. Lucky for me, her writing's messy — none of those loops and squiggles like some girls have.

"Todd had another headache so we kept him home yesterday afternoon. Thank you for understanding. Yours truly, Cecilia Lerner." I check it over for spelling mistakes (Cooper would be impressed) and tuck it into the side pocket of my backpack.

I settle up with Rick before I leave school. When no one's looking, I pass him an envelope with the cash in it — plus the interest. He actually seems a little disappointed. I guess he liked knowing I owed him money.

The minute I leave the building, I phone Edgar Milne and tell him I've got his money, too. "I'm glad to hear it, Todd," he says. When we meet at this coffee shop near my parents' office, he's just what I expected: a tall, thin guy in a grey pinstripe suit. I give him his envelope. I'm a little concerned he might want to get into a conversation (what in the world would we have to talk about?), but luckily, that doesn't happen. Instead, he uses the tip of his index finger to count the money, then gives me a stern look.

"It's all there," I say.

"I can see that. But aren't you supposed to be in school this afternoon?"

* * *

My next stop is les Cours Mont-Royal. It's a good thing I got here today, because as the saleslady — not the same one who was here last time — explains, this is their last pair of Chanel sunglasses.

"Are they for someone special?" she asks as she slides them into a gold brocade bag.

"As a matter of fact, they're for my girlfriend."

Claire isn't officially my girlfriend. But I'm hoping that when I give her the sunglasses, she will be.

* * *

On the métro home, I get this incredible feeling of well-being. It's true the air down here smells of stale fumes; a baby in my métro car won't stop wailing, and his mom isn't doing anything about it. Still, I feel good. Very good. One more envelope to deliver to Patrick tomorrow, and I'll be debt free.

When I get off the métro, I pass a flower shop on Laurier Street. On an impulse, I turn back and walk in. "I'll take that bouquet," I tell the guy who works there, pointing to a bunch of colourful flowers in a vase near the cash. They're for my mom. After all, she let me take the afternoon off school, didn't she?

* * *

I still have 40 minutes till my next errand, so I bring the flowers back to the condo and put them in water. Olive doesn't hear me come in. She's busy mopping up after the workers. I can hear her talking to herself as she works. "This plaster dust will be the end of me," she mutters.

When I check my watch, I realize it's time to get going. School's out in fifteen minutes and I want to meet Claire at the corner near her house. When I pick up the small bag containing her sunglasses, I get another burst of that good feeling I had in the métro. Is this what falling in love feels like?

I can see Claire walking down the street towards

me. She's swinging her purse with one hand. I watch as she stops to pet a black cat. In the afternoon sun, her hair looks almost white. It's not till she gets a little closer that I notice the sunglasses.

The thing is, I'm getting to be kind of an expert on expensive sunglasses. I can tell right away that those are Chanels.

She bought them already.

"Hey Todd!" Claire waves when she spots me. "How come you weren't in school this afternoon?"

"Oh, you know, I had a little business to take care of."

"Don't you think it's a bad idea to skip classes like that?" Claire's voice sounds disappointed, but her body language is telling me something different. She moves up close to me and, for a second, her hand brushes against mine. Sparks that feel like electricity shoot up from my feet straight to my thighs.

"Nice sunglasses," I say, tucking the bag from les Cours under my arm so she won't see it.

Claire giggles. "I couldn't take it anymore. So I went ahead and bought them. I figure I'll deal with my dad when he gets the bill."

"They look good," I say.

When Claire smiles, she looks like a movie star. "I know," she says, and then she giggles some more. "I bumped into Rick Lee just now — when I was leaving school. He said he loves them on me."

I can't believe how quickly a person can go from feeling great to feeling rotten. I could offer to walk Claire home, but I don't really want to. I feel like an idiot, and all I want to do right now is lie on my bed and forget I ever met Claire.

On my way home, I can only think of one thing that might cheer me up: a card game. I know I shouldn't go back to the online casino, but it feels like the site is calling to me, like those mermaids that sing to sailors over the sound of the waves. "Luring them to their destruction," I can hear Cooper saying. But I don't care. All I know is that right now, thinking of cards is helping me take my mind off my lousy life.

As I use my key to open the door to the condo, I'm already picturing myself in front of my computer, logging on to the site. It's only four, so Olive will have left and my parents won't be home for hours.

But when I open the door, I hear voices coming from the living room. It's my mom and dad. What are they doing home? My first thought is that that nerdy Mr. Milne ratted me out.

I take a deep breath and walk into the living room. What's Mark doing here?

"Todd," my mother says. "Your brother is having a bit of a crisis. The university sent him home."

When I turn to look at him, my brother turns away.

Chapter 25

Mark is slumped on the couch, looking like a balloon that's had all the air taken out of it.

"What the hell is going on?" I ask from the doorway where I'm standing. My parents are sitting on a pair of matching armchairs, facing Mark. My mom chews her bottom lip.

"He says he doesn't want to talk about it," my father says.

"Leave him be," my mother tells my father. "The important thing is we're all together."

Yeah right. All together means we eat lasagna in the dining room. Only nobody says anything — or at least anything that's important. When my mom asks Mark whether he's made any friends at school, my dad changes the subject. "How's the weather been in Boston lately?" he asks Mark.

Mark picks at a piece of garlic bread. "Fine," he says, without looking up.

It's a relief when, just before dessert, my cell phone rings. "Mind if I get that? I'll keep it short," I tell my parents as I get up from the table and head into the kitchen. I know from my caller ID it's Claire.

"What's up?" I try to sound casual.

"I ... uh ... just wanted to make sure everything was okay with you — with us." I can tell she's embarrassed.

"Everything's fine."

"You seemed upset before. I thought maybe it was about the sunglasses."

"I wasn't."

"You sure?"

I shift from one foot to the other. "Look, my brother just came home unexpectedly. How about I call you later — or we talk in school tomorrow?"

"Wanna do something Saturday night?" she asks before she hangs up.

I nearly say, "Why don't you see if Rick is free on Saturday night?" But then I picture Claire kneeling down to pet that black cat. "Okay," I say instead.

When I get back to the table, my brother glares at me. "Did you have to say that about me coming home unexpectedly?"

I glare back at him. "No one told me it was a state secret."

* * *

The first thing I do when I get to my room is turn on the computer. An icon pops up to tell me there's mail. It's probably spam, but I check it just the same. I'll get online as soon as I'm done.

But it's not spam. It's from Mark, which is kind of weird, since he's never emailed me before. I check the date and the time. Did he send it yesterday from Boston? No, he sent it just now, from down the hall. Talk about weird.

"You wanted to know what was up. So here it is: I've been expelled from MIT for cheating. Basically, I've blown my chances there, and also that summer internship I had lined up. The thing is, I don't have the heart to tell Mom and Dad. But I figure since you always resented me for being the family genius, you're the one person who'd be glad to hear the news. Signed, your brother Mark."

I can't believe what I just read. So I read it over. Twice. Then I hit reply: "Why in the world would a guy like you cheat on an exam?"

About four seconds later, the answer pops up. It's just one word: "Pressure."

Mark's right that I've always resented him for being the family genius. But he's wrong about my being glad to hear he's in trouble. So instead of going to the poker website like I was planning to, I walk across the condo and knock on Mark's door.

* * *

He doesn't seem surprised to see me. He's lying on his bed, staring up at the ceiling.

"Was that some chick who phoned you before?" he asks. Coming from him, the word "chick" sounds wrong. Like he's trying to be cool.

"What does that have to do with anything?"

"Well, was it?"

"Yeah, as a matter of fact it was."

"Do you like her?" He's still lying on his bed, but I guess this counts as a conversation — or as close to a conversation as the two of us have got since we were little kids watching Saturday morning cartoons while our parents slept in.

"Yeah, I like her. Why do you want to know?" I'm starting to think Mark's losing it. He's never shown any interest in my personal life before. Not that I've ever given much thought to his either. The fact is, Mark's never had much of a personal life. No best friend, no girlfriend, nothing. But what do you expect from a guy who emails his brother from down the hall?

"Making friends is easy for you." Mark makes it sound like an accusation.

"Well you must have a couple of friends, don't you?"

"Not really ..." He's practically whispering now.

"Huh? Not one?" There's an uncomfortable silence and for a second, I'm sorry I asked.

"Look," Mark says at last, "I know someone like you might find this hard to believe, but no, I don't have one friend. Not one. I just study all the time. And then I reached this point where I couldn't study anymore. I couldn't do anything. I couldn't even sleep."

It's hard for me to imagine what studying all the time feels like. But I know how bad not sleeping feels. I think back to the night I lost the thousand bucks online. "That sucks," I say.

Mark stares some more at the ceiling. I get the feeling he wants something from me. Something bigger than my sympathy.

"What do I do wrong?" he asks. His voice sounds small, like it's coming from far away.

I suck in my breath. It's hard to believe Mr. Wonderful is asking *me* what *he* does wrong. But maybe he's on to something. Maybe I do know something Mark doesn't. Maybe I know about making friends. I never thought about it before, that's for sure. It just comes naturally. Like computers come naturally to Mark. Like business deals come naturally to my mom and dad.

"Look," I tell him, "it might help if you didn't talk about school and how great you are all the time."

"Do I do that?" He sounds surprised.

"Based on my observations, I'd say yes. Definitely yes. And you shouldn't use the word 'chick.' It doesn't sound right when you say it."

Mark nods his head slowly. Then for a few seconds, neither of us says a word.

"What'd you mean about pressure?" I finally ask.

This time, Mark turns to face me. "I've been under tremendous pressure for a while now. I want to make Mom and Dad happy, I want them to be

151

proud of me, but the competition at MIT is unbelievable. I just can't keep up anymore. And the thing is — not having a social life is starting to get to me. I think that's why I cheated."

"You cheated because you don't have friends?" I'm having trouble following his logic.

"I cheated because I can't go on like this anymore."

I nod my head in the dark. "When are you gonna tell Mom and Dad?"

"When I'm ready." Mark stares back up into space. "Hey little brother," he says, addressing the ceiling, "who ever thought you'd turn out to be the well-adjusted one in this family?"

The thought makes Mark laugh. I laugh too — partly because I'm glad to hear him laugh, but also because it's funny. Way funnier than he knows.

* * *

By the time I get back to my room, I'm too tired to shut down the computer. So I crawl into bed. As I drift off, the sound of Mark's laughter echoes in my head — "Who ever thought you'd turn out to be the well-adjusted one?"

Of course I know the truth. I'm not at all well-adjusted. Sure, I have friends; sure, I have an almost-girlfriend, but I've also been selling counterfeit money to thirteen-year-olds. The sleep button on my computer flickers in the dark. Which makes me think about gambling online, and playing poker with Rick and his friends, and the casino, and all the money I owed.

How well-adjusted is a guy hooked on gambling?

Chapter 26

"What's this?" Patrick asks when he's through counting the money. His dark eyes look like they've become even darker. "You were gonna pay me six bucks a bill."

"That was before I knew they all had the same serial number."

Patrick looks up at me for a second, then away. "Okay, man," he mutters, "I'll settle for five."

"Four," I say, "not a cent more."

"You drive a hard bargain, kid. Next time, we'll be more careful about them serial numbers." Them numbers. Old Patrick needs a little work in the grammar department.

"I don't think there's gonna be a next time," I tell him. "I'm thinking about cleaning up my act."

Patrick claps my back. "We all think about it. We just never get around to doing it."

* * *

A window washer is emptying a pail of dirty water into a drain on Laurier Street. I catch my reflection in one of the freshly cleaned windows. As I examine my reflection, I'm reminded of . Cooper's assignment. *Who in the world am I, anyway?*

I wonder how Mark would answer the question. I never thought I'd actually catch myself feeling sorry for my big brother, but I do. Mr. Wonderful isn't so wonderful after all. But if Mark's not the person I thought he was, doesn't that make me a different person, too? Cooper was right about one thing: the identity can get pretty complicated.

A group of kids in Hilltop uniforms are leaving the magazine store up ahead. The store entrance is narrow, so they're shouting and shoving each other. "Move!" one of them yells. "You're giving me claustrophobia!" When he turns around, I realize he's the curly-haired seventh-grader who bought some of my phony bills. Once he's on the sidewalk, he stops to tear the plastic wrapper from a pack of cigarettes.

"How much cash you got on you?" one of the other kids asks him.

"Over a hundred," he answers. "But I have to keep enough to buy fake ID."

Fake ID in Grade 7? We got them back in Grade 9, but this kid can't be serious. No bouncer in the city would let a thirteen-year-old into a club. Especially not one this kid's size.

"Fake ID?" His friend seems interested. "How much you paying?"

I slow down, observing the seventh-graders from a distance, until they go into a convenience store. They seem to travel in a pack. "Let's see if they'll sell us some beer," one boy says, pulling some bills from his front pocket. Something tells me I'd probably recognize the serial number on those babies. Cigarettes, fake ID, beer. Nice to know the money I sold them's going to a good cause.

* * *

I use my cell phone to call Lewis. I've been kind of out of it lately, distracted by the crap I've been going through, but now I've got this urge to reconnect with my old life. Before things turned complicated. Maybe Lewis'll want to hang out.

But when he picks up, he doesn't sound all that happy to hear from me.

"Look," he says, "I'm kind of busy. I'll call you back af-sher supper, okay?"

For a second, I don't know what to say. In all the years I've known him, Lewis has never once been too busy to talk to me — and I've never heard him slur his words. Could he be drinking?

"I'll call you back af-sher supper," he says again. Why is he repeating himself?

Something is definitely wrong. What could Lewis be up to on a Friday afternoon that he wouldn't want me to know about? As soon as I ask myself the question, the answer pops into my head. He's at Rick's house.

* * *

I jog, so I'm there in less than ten minutes. Lewis's ten-speed is parked outside, locked up to a fence post.

At first, no one answers the doorbell. Then I notice some movement behind the living room curtains. A minute later, Rick comes to the door, opening it just a sliver.

"Look man," he says, "I'm sorry I didn't invite you to play cards today. We've got a full table. Eight guys." Rick starts to close the door on me.

The weird part is, for once in my life, I'm not thinking about gambling. I'm not imagining winning hands or piles of chips. I'm focused on Lewis. But now, with Rick trying to shut the door on me, I'm starting to feel insulted. Maybe I do want to gamble. After all, it's not like I need a loan. The old urge is coming back, creeping up on me like foggy weather.

Rick presses against the door. Why is he trying so hard to get rid of me? That's when I realize what's going on — Rick and his friends must be trying to con Lewis out of his money. And Lewis was probably so happy to be invited to their poker game, he fell for it.

I lift my hand and plant it on the door frame so

Rick won't be able to shut the door. "I want to talk to Lewis."

"Who are you — his mother?"

Loud laughter comes from the dining room. But I don't hear Lewis laughing.

"Lewis!" I call out, raising my voice so he'll hear me. "I need to talk to you!"

A stocky Asian guy I've never seen comes to the front door.

"Is there a problem here?" he asks. When he opens his mouth, I smell beer on his breath.

For a second, I think about turning away. If Lewis wants to gamble away his money, it's his business. Besides, the stocky guy looks like a sumo wrestler itching for a fight.

Still, I can't shake the feeling I'm somehow responsible for Lewis. After all, I'm the one who taught him how to play Texas Hold 'em. If it weren't for me, he'd be home helping his sister with her math homework.

"Lewis!" I say, pushing my way past Rick. That's when the sumo wrestler grabs me by the collar. For a second, I'm sure he's going to hit me. And when he does, I know it's going to hurt bad. Real bad. This guy is massive. He could break bones without even trying.

"Let go of me!" The sound of my own voice catches me by surprise. It's not that I yelled. In fact, I didn't even raise my voice. The surprising thing is that I sounded sure of myself, focused. Like I meant business.

I'm even more surprised when the sumo wrestler releases his grip.

Lewis is slumped over the dining room table. There are five empty beer bottles on the table in front of him.

"Come on Lew," I say as I head for where he's sitting, "it's time to go home."

"I want to go all in. All in," Lewis says, reaching for his pile of chips.

"No he doesn't," I say, putting my hand over Lewis's. "Lewis wants to cash out. Now."

The other guys aren't too happy about it, but they cash him out — to the tune of $130. "I'll look after that for you," I tell Lewis, taking the money out of his hands and stashing it in my front pocket.

It's not easy getting Lewis out of his chair and then out of the house. "I was doing fine," he mutters as I lead him down Rick's front stairs.

Just as we get to the last stair, Lewis falls over. Now I need to find some way to lift him up. I take his weight on my shoulder and hoist him up. He really needs to lose a few pounds.

"My bike's over there," Lewis says, gesturing towards the fence.

"I don't think you're ready to ride a bike." Then I take a deep breath and get ready to start hauling him down the street to my house.

Chapter 27

Mark raises an eyebrow when Lewis and I walk into the condo.

"You shoulda let me go all in," Lewis mutters. He's been babbling the whole way back, and it's starting to annoy me.

My whole body — even the skin behind my knees — is dripping with sweat. I don't think I've worked so hard in my life.

"Why don't you give it a rest, Lew?" I say as I help him take off his shoes. I take the $130 from my pocket and hand it to him. "Just be glad you didn't gamble away your lawn mowing money."

Lewis burps.

When Mark gets up from the kitchen stool where he's been sitting and opens the fridge door, I think he's about to make himself a sandwich. Then I notice he's got a bag of coffee in his hands.

"Thanks," I say as he pours water into the coffee

machine. As the sharp smell of coffee fills the air, my shoulder muscles finally begin to relax.

* * *

Claire takes me to see *Ghostkiller*. It's a stupid movie, but I like how she holds onto my elbow during the scary parts.

"So do you think I was wrong to buy those sunglasses without checking with my dad first?" she asks on the way home.

At first, I don't say anything. "Some things are hard to resist."

"I went way over my monthly budget," Claire says. "Do you think I should return them?" For a moment, she sounds like she's seven years old.

"I don't know, Claire. You have to figure it out."

Neither of us says anything as we walk down the block towards her house.

"I know it sounds bad, but I really like those sunglasses," Claire says when we get to her front stairs.

"There's also this amazing pair of Seven jeans I really really want. You should see the fit." Her voice gets kind of breathless as she describes the jeans. "But they're $300. My dad'll freak."

For the first time, I'm starting to feel like maybe I don't like Claire as much as I thought I did. When she lifts her chin up so I can kiss her — I only brush my lips against hers for a second.

"Oh my God," Claire says, just as I'm turning

around to head home. "I can't believe I almost forgot to tell you this, Todd. A bunch of kids from Grade 7 got caught today using counterfeit money. Where do you think they got it?"

"Beats me," I say, stopping on the flagstone path that leads from Claire's house to the sidewalk. After Claire lets herself in, I wait on the path till my heart stops racing.

* * *

I'm jumpy all day Sunday, and my stomach feels queasy. When, on my way to school on Monday morning, I spot a row of police cruisers parked outside the building, I feel like I'm going to puke.

"You're looking a little peaked again," Cooper tells me when I walk into English class. "Too much partying this weekend?"

"Something like that," I say, trying to smile.

It's impossible to concentrate in class. Every ten minutes, I spot another Grade 7 student walking down the hall to the headmaster's office. That's where the police must be doing their interviews.

I try to figure out the best strategy. I can intercept one of the kids on his way to the office, intimidate him a little, remind him of the trouble he'll be in if he snitches on me. Or I can lie low and hope no one gives me away. I don't have to look down at my hands to know they're trembling.

In the end, I decide it's better not to draw too much attention to myself. After class, I stay clear of the headmaster's office. When the recess bell goes, I force myself to head for the computer lab. I've gotta do something — anything — to keep my mind off my situation. Besides, I have work to do on my website.

Everywhere I look — in the hallway, near the lockers — students seem to be hanging out in little groups, whispering. Every so often, someone points towards the front of the school, where the police cars are still parked.

When I breathe, my chest feels like there's too much air in it. Am I starting to hyperventilate or something? I tell myself to breathe in and out slowly. If I can relax, I'll be okay. Everything'll be okay. Won't it?

I feel a little calmer when I open the door to the computer lab. I try to focus on my plans for the website. For the first time, I think maybe I shouldn't just give tips to help kids win when they gamble. Maybe it wouldn't be so bad if I also came up with a few tips to help stop them from getting hooked. After all, if I'd read something like that, maybe I wouldn't be in the mess I'm in now.

* * *

Even though the cop cars are gone by the time I leave school, I can't help looking over my shoulder. But there's no one coming after me. I take a slow, deep breath. Maybe, just maybe, I've managed to get away with it.

Still, I'm feeling jumpy. Every time I turn a corner, I half expect someone to pop out and stop me. Later, at home, I start sweating every time the phone rings. But it's only the dentist's office calling to say it's time for my annual checkup, and the painter leaving a message for my mom.

The four of us are eating pizza in the den when the doorbell rings. I wipe the tomato sauce from my face as my dad gets up from the couch to see who's there.

For a second, it feels to me like he's moving in slow motion. With every step he takes, random pictures go through my head. It's like I'm watching a disjointed movie. I see the beautiful girls on the gambling website; Lewis falling outside Rick's house; the Grade 7 kids hoping to buy beer at the convenience store; and Patrick counting his money.

I hear voices coming from the hallway, but the sounds are muffled — as if they're coming from underwater. But every few seconds, I hear my name. My hands feel so cold that I start rubbing them together for warmth.

I know it's the police even before one of the officers steps into the den and introduces himself.

"Sergeant Gagnon," he says, and I notice the gun hanging from his belt. "We'd like to talk to Todd Lerner." He looks from Mark to me.

I've never noticed before how lined my father's face is.

"What in God's name is going on, Todd?"

I can feel the sergeant's eyes on me.

Silently, I get up from the couch. Mark is watching me, too. At first, I think he feels bad for me. Last night, he told my parents what really happened at MIT — so now he knows what it feels like to disappoint them. But when my eyes meet Mark's, I see something besides sympathy. He's relieved. Relieved I've made an even bigger mess than he has. That if the police are here, my crime has got to be way worse than his.

My legs wobble as I step towards the two cops. At first, I drop my head, but then I lift it so I'm looking right at the sergeant.

My mom moves over to block my way. Her hand's over her mouth like she can't handle any more bad news. Then she drops her hand and turns to the cops.

"My son would never do anything illegal," she insists, but from the way her voice is quivering, I can tell she's not sure that's true.

"We have information linking you to a counterfeiting operation at Hilltop Academy," the other officer tells me. Though he only says it once, his voice echoes in my head: *We have information linking you to a counterfeiting operation at Hilltop Academy.*

My mom gasps. My father spins to face me and raises one finger to his lips. Except for his eyes, which look like they've caught fire, everything else about him seems calm.

"Don't say anything, Todd," he says, his lips tight. "Not until we've talked to Lewis's father."

My dad will be angry, but I know one thing: I can't not say anything. I've had it with secrets. I've had it with poker faces.

"I am responsible," I say. When I hear myself speak, I can't quite believe how strong and clear my voice sounds.

My father grabs my wrist, but I shake it loose. Yes, I'm in trouble. Yes, I'll have to pay the price for the stuff I've done wrong. I'll probably get kicked out of Hilltop — and who knows if there's another school in Montreal that'll take me?

But for the first time in fifteen years, I feel like I'm starting — just starting — to know who I am.